LOCKDOWN

YOU'VE BEEN PLANNING TO LEAVE YOUR
HUSBAND. NOW THERE'S NO ESCAPE...

MARIA FRANKLAND

AUTONOMY
PRESS

First published by Autonomy Press 2024

First edition

Cover Design by David Grogan www.headdesign.co.uk

For Michael and Matthew - my almost-perfect lockdown companions

PROLOGUE

'IT WAS NEVER GOING to end well,' the woman standing closest to me mutters to no one in particular.

I nod at what she's saying. We've all glimpsed the shadows of suffering in this ill-fated house as we've passed by it. We've all contributed to the whispers surrounding the dysfunction that's existed behind those closed doors.

And now this latest rumour, the one we're all braced for – the prospect of at least one dead body lying in there. Yet another thing to haunt our minds as we return to being locked inside our homes.

A chilling hush has fallen over those of us gathered here, only permeated by the wail of another approaching siren. We keep our distance from one another as best we can, communicating only through wide-eyed glances. Suddenly the threat of a Covid infection doesn't seem as significant as what the police are about to uncover behind those curtained windows.

'Return to your homes.' A voice, stern and commanding, shatters the uneasy quiet.

But nobody budges. A second voice is drowned out by the deafening thud of the battering ram as it crashes once, twice, then three times against the door.

As officers shout to one another from behind their masks, all we can do is watch as helplessly as we have been forced to all along.

The force of each strike reverberates through my body, causing shivers of dread.

After the fourth strike, there's an audible gasp as the door yields with a final, resounding crash against the hallway wall. As the police surge into the house, we collectively hold our breath.

MELISSA

1

'YOU SHOULD PROBABLY GET MOVING on this.' Annie squints, her eyes narrowing against the early afternoon sunlight. 'The headlines are saying we could end up like Italy and be forced into some kind of lockdown within the next few days.'

We're on our own out here in the beer garden. Many people appear to have taken to hiding in their houses over the last few days. A subtle tension grips me, reminding me that I should be retreating indoors as well.

'As if I haven't enough to cope with right now.' Momentarily lost in thought, I study the stitching on my dress. 'It's all such a bloody mess.'

'I *did* try to warn you about him, Melissa. Time and time again, in fact.' She slides a band from her wrist and twists her hair into a bun. 'Gosh, it's boiling out here. It feels more like July than March. It's nice to get my sandals back on though.'

I nod. It *is* warm. However, I won't be taking my cardigan off. If she were to see the bruises on my arms, she'd have a fit.

'Don't be an *I told you so*,' I say with a sigh, avoiding her gaze. What she's said is perfectly true. - she *did* tell me to be careful with Justin – a warning she repeated at every turn.

She never knew his ex-wife but has heard many stories about when they were together from my next-door-but-one neighbour, Diane. These stories haven't only been relayed through this one neighbour – a couple of the others have offered their accounts to Annie throughout the eighteen months she's lived in the area. She often jokes that hearing all the gossip is both a blessing and a curse but part and parcel of living above a pub.

I dismissed all warnings about the possessiveness and violence in Justin's former marriage as rumours his ex-wife herself must have concocted and spread around.

In the two years of being with him, the spectre of Lynette has lingered, always a sign of the storm brewing beneath our seemingly idyllic surface, yet a sign I didn't take any notice of. The tale Justin always spun was that Lynette would stop at nothing to bring him down, especially while they were separating. He talked about how she'd single-handledly turned everyone, including their son, against him with her lies and exaggerations. I was selective in what I chose to believe, filtering his narrative to fit the version I wanted to hear.

From what he told me, it sounded like one of the most acrimonious divorces there could be, and in the beginning, although I wanted to keep well out of it all, I couldn't help but feel sorry for him.

Our online connection sparked a magnetic attraction. Little did I know, that pull concealed a darker force, waiting to unravel before my eyes. All I'd ever known about Justin, in the beginning, was his attentiveness and the spontaneous fun we had together. Bouquets of flowers and surprise weekend breaks became our norm and he was always springing surprises on me. Once, while the kids were with Rick, and I was cooking me and Justin a special three-course meal, I wondered why he was so quiet. It turned out, he was booking us a romantic break in Paris. It was one of the happiest weekends I've ever spent.

Then, so the kids wouldn't feel left out, he booked a long

weekend in a seaside lodge. While we were there, he continually badgered me to move into his house with my kids when we got back. As I watched him building sandcastles with Ewan and Aisla, I realised I was running out of reasons not to.

Then, bit by bit, his mask began to slip. In the end, there was nothing for him to hide behind, and I was able to see exactly who he was.

'I'm sorry - I don't mean to sound so preachy.' Annie's eyes are sympathetic as she sighs. 'I just wish you'd listened to me sooner. Especially before you—' Her voice trails off as she nods toward my rapidly expanding belly. She doesn't need to say any more.

'It's not just *you* I should have listened to.' I drain the last of my tea. 'A couple of the neighbours *directly* asked me if I had any idea what I was getting into.'

My mind returns to our moving-in day when I was first cornered by Diane. There was a darkness in her face as she suggested I didn't have a clue who I was planning to marry. I'd responded angrily, telling her to mind her own business.

Then I'd headed inside to join Justin. He was pouring champagne to celebrate our new beginning. There was absolutely no sign of this man Diane was trying to warn me about. And it *was* a new beginning, we were deliriously happy.

At least, we were to start with.

2

'IF YOU'D LISTENED, you could have saved yourself a year of being so unhappily married.' Despite the apology she's just made, Annie's not letting the *I told you so* conversation go. 'Not to mention,' she continues. 'All this upheaval and hassle you're now having to face – at a time when you should be putting your feet up.'

'It hasn't been a year though, has it? Things were mostly OK between us until Christmas,' I say. 'Or I wouldn't be in *this* predicament.' I bring my hands down to rest on my midriff.

'Ah, come on Melissa, you know that's not true.' Annie fiddles with the stem of her wine glass. 'Even last summer, you were complaining how he was spending more time *here* than he did at home.'

'I know I did. But there *was* another side to him, you know. A nicer side. Even now, I still occasionally get a glimmer of what he was like before we moved in together.'

'That's just part of the control he has over you.'

'If I were still so under his control, I wouldn't be about to leave, would I?'

'You should have done it months ago.'

'I was too busy blaming myself for it all. Too busy wondering if I was doing something to make him this way.'

'I know. Thank God I managed to talk some sense into you. It's better late than never anyway. The sooner you get out of there, the better.'

'Alright Annie, can we talk about something else now?'

However, she's on a roll. 'The way he behaved in front of your kids should have been the last straw,' she says. 'He completely ruined Christmas for all of you.'

I can't argue with her. Because Cameron, Justin's son, had refused to speak to him when he'd tried to call him, he'd ended up in a drunken, stinking, black mood and I couldn't do anything to pacify him. The kids were terrified – I ended up having to ship them off to their dad's house, after fighting tooth and nail to be able to have them with me on Christmas Day. The plan had originally been to drop them off with Rick on Boxing Day.

'I *do* wish I'd listened to you. But sometimes, it takes time for someone to show you their true colours.'

'You saw what you wanted to see, I guess.'

Something in her tone completely deflates me. I keep making excuses for why I didn't leave the moment he showed me what he was capable of, but really, there aren't any.

'Stupid,' I whisper, almost to myself, as the weight of my poor choices settles more heavily on my shoulders. I look at Annie. 'It's not just me I've affected, is it? I've managed to drag my poor kids into all this.' I brush a tear away.

'Hey, I'm sorry. I didn't mean for you to start getting upset.'

'You should see them, Annie.' Each attempt to brush away the tears only accelerates their flow. 'Every time he puts his key in the lock, fear is written all over their faces.'

I tug a tissue from my bag and dab at my eyes. Then I look around where we're sitting. Every time I talk about Justin, I have a weird fear that he's going to be secretly listening and will pop out from somewhere. He's at work this morning so it's clearly an *irrational* fear.

'It's alright. He's not going to suddenly jump out from behind a tree.' It's as if she's read my mind.

'Aisla normally scarpers upstairs but poor Ewan seems to think it's his job to protect me. I feel so bloody guilty. And now there's going to be another one to think of.'

'You're doing something about it *now*. That's the main thing.' Annie reaches across the table for my hand. I sharply tug mine out of the way.

'It's alright.' She laughs but looks mildly hurt by my rebuff. 'I don't have the lurgy.'

'*You're* more likely to catch it than *anyone*,' I reply. 'All those sick patients you look after.'

'We've only had two cases at our hospital so far - and they haven't needed to be brought into intensive care.'

'Are they still in isolation?'

'Of course. Don't worry – I haven't been anywhere near them.'

'I hear what you're saying, but I've got to be careful with being pregnant, haven't I? And then there's my asthma.' As if to reassure myself, I feel in my bag for my inhaler. 'Call me paranoid but—'

'You'll be fine. We're sitting *outside*, aren't we? And there've been *no* cases in Otley so far. *Not one*. We might not even get it here, if everyone's careful and keeps washing their hands.'

'Still.' I clasp my hands together beneath the table in case Annie gets any ideas about grabbing them again. Being so touchy-feely must be part and parcel of being a nurse. 'The whole thing scares me to death – I'm just so stressed.'

'It's no wonder. Can I get you another cuppa?' She nods towards my mug and picks up her empty wine glass.

I push it towards her. 'Go on then. Just a quick one.'

Annie rises from the table and looks up into the clear blue sky. 'I wish my work would send *me* home until further notice while the weather's like this.'

'I'd rather be working and for everything to be back to normal.' It's true. When I'm at my perch at the hotel reception desk, I can almost pretend real life doesn't exist beyond it.' I reach towards my purse. 'Do you want me to get these?'

'Don't be so daft.' She reaches for my mug. 'There might as well be some perks to being married to the landlord.'

I stare after her as she heads towards the rear door. Her mention of Simon reminds me of how lousy I feel for not telling her what I know about him. But what he's done does seem to have been a drunken one-off, so I don't want to be the one to blow Annie's world apart so soon after they've got married. Certainly not at the moment, with the added pressure of the virus.

I'll definitely be taking him to one side when I get the chance though. I want him to know that I know. He needs to be in no doubt that if he's *ever* unfaithful to my friend again, I won't hesitate to tell her next time.

The distant laughter of children echoes through the air, a reminder of how much I'm missing my own two. I wish I could go and collect them – many other parents seem to be keeping theirs at home today. The only reason I haven't is because I'm supposed to be spending this afternoon moving our stuff into the new place, so I need them well out of the way.

According to the headlines, it's only a matter of time before the schools are all closed anyway - and from what I heard on the news an hour ago, it sounds like it could be as soon as today.

My hand instinctively seeks my phone for what feels like the millionth time since I got up this morning, firstly hitting the refresh button on my email and then checking my call log – still nothing. I continue to stare at the screen as though that will magically bring forth the call I'm waiting for. *Come on, come on.* I will it to ring - I just need to hear the words, *the keys are ready for you,* and then I can get on with it all.

Like I told the agent last week, I don't need them to check the place, clean it, or whatever else they usually do - I just need those keys as soon as humanly possible. He gave me his word it would be today. Yet today's ticking on and it's after two o'clock already.

Trying to steady my breathing, I stare at the tree in the corner of the beer garden, its blossom shimmering in the barely-there breeze. The sun-drenched day, with its cloudless sky, offers little solace to my sombre mood – if anything, it makes me feel even more miserable about how everything's gone wrong. And my anxiety levels are through the roof as I wait for news of those keys.

The desire to share a glass of wine with Annie tugs at me – if only to settle me down, but it's another five months until I'll be able to enjoy one of those.

I know what I've got to do, but doing it *successfully,* not to mention *safely,* is another matter. If it gets much later in the day, I'll be forced to postpone our move until tomorrow. Justin will be home in less than four hours, unless he ends up here, in the pub, in which case it could be six or seven. But I've no way of knowing, and I can't risk him catching me in the act of leaving.

I'll have this last cuppa with Annie – after all, it's not as if I can do much until I get the keys. I've got our packing boxes hidden in the loft and the number for a man with a van ready in my phone – I just pray he's still available at such short notice. I've told him I'm pregnant and he's happy to do all the lifting for me. What he's got no idea about are the circumstances I'm running from – perhaps he'd be reluctant to get involved if he knew.

The move will be a huge shock for Aisla and Ewan when I collect them from the after-school club, but Annie's right – I *do* need to get going on this. I check my phone again.

The sunshine catches the glitter that Aisla painted onto my nails last week. I haven't had my nails done properly for ages - I haven't even visited the hairdresser for my usual highlights since before Christmas. Instead, every spare penny has gone into my escape fund. I've done well to get a deposit and a month's rent in advance together without Justin noticing.

However, as Annie's already tried to warn me, *the most dangerous time is often just before you leave.*

For my sake, the kids' sakes and the baby's, I need to be really careful.

'Melissa.' Annie's voice is a hiss as she scoots from the pub door and back towards me. Her face is dark and full of worry. 'He's just turned up.'

3

'Who?'

She jerks her head back towards the pub. 'Justin. Can't you hear him?'

She stops dead in front of me. Sure enough, though the words are muffled, the tone of Justin's furious shouts is unmistakable.

'He's supposed to be at work,' I whisper.

'Apparently, he's been fired - that's as much as I caught from what he was saying.' She places my replenished mug in front of me. I attempt to lift it, but my trembling hands betray the fear pulsating through me.

'So I've left Simon to deal with him.'

'He's lost yet another job?' I shake my head, feeling the weight of my tangled hair brushing against my cheeks. 'Though I can't say I'm all that surprised.'

'Was he still on his final warning?' She sits facing me again.

'He's been on a final written warning for months – no employer tolerates someone who's consistently absent, do they?' Normally, I'd be worrying about how we're going to manage, but since I'm leaving, it's no longer going to be my problem.

'Simon said he's a bit work-shy. Is he still as bad?'

'Oh yes.' I smile, despite how stressed I'm feeling. 'In the rare occasions he does bother going in, he's *always* late. I thought things were going to be easier, you know, being able to pool our resources when we moved in together. But I've ended up even more broke than I was on my own.' I exhale a jagged breath.

'Are you OK?'

'Just stressed.' I tilt my phone screen towards my face. 'I needed him out of the way.'

'There's going to be some sort of announcement from the government any time soon – it could even be today.' Annie wipes lipstick from the edge of her glass. 'We could even be stopped from leaving our houses like what's happening in Italy.'

A vision of the deserted Italian streets they've shown on the news enters my mind. 'I can't see it getting to that. I know the virus is a massive worry, but things aren't nearly as bad *here* as they are in Europe.' As I speak, I'm trying to convince myself as much as Annie.

'No matter what happens Melissa,' she adopts a firmer tone. 'You've *got* to get yourself and those kids out of that house.'

'I'm trying, aren't I?' I can't take my eyes off the door. If Justin notices me out here, he'll burst through that door and start carrying on. I always get the brunt of anything that goes wrong in his life. He usually tones it down in front of other people so maybe I'll be safer here. However, judging from how he's carrying on in there right now, he seems to no longer care about how he might be perceived.

'Is there still nothing from the agent?' Annie nods towards my phone.

'No. He'll still be waiting for the previous tenants to hand the keys back in. They're supposed to have posted them back through the agency door over the weekend.'

'I think you should be chasing the agent *now*. God, if only Simon hadn't already let that flat go to someone else.' She nods her head in the direction of the block of flats, several doors down. 'But the woman will have already signed the lease – she's supposed to be moving in today.'

'It wouldn't have been any good for us.' Despite my words, I try to keep an element of gratitude in my voice. Annie is, after all, only trying to help me. 'It literally overlooks the house from which we're escaping!'

'True.' She looks thoughtful. 'But you'd still be out of the same four walls as *him*. Honestly Melissa, I'm really worried about you all, especially after what you've been telling me lately.'

'Keep your voice down.' I nod in the direction of the pub. 'Look, we'll be OK.' I attempt to load a conviction I'm not feeling into my voice. 'I've just about got everything lined up, haven't I? All I can do now is wait for the green light from the agent.'

'You know you can stay here if there are any hold-ups. I promise not to breathe on you when I'm coming off a shift.' She laughs, though we both know what's going on is far from funny.

'From what I've read, I'm classed as vulnerable, and should be distancing myself completely – they're calling it shielding. But I need to get into the new house before I can do that.'

I certainly shouldn't be *here*. But I don't say this. If the truth be known, without the children or work to keep me occupied, I've been climbing the walls this morning while waiting for the agent to call. I didn't need asking twice when Annie messaged me, inviting me over for a cuppa.

'Yeah, there are quite a few people who should be shielding.'

'I'm trying not to be but I *am* really scared of catching the virus. Perhaps my inhalers wouldn't even work against it.'

'Well, I meant what I said.' She tucks a stray hair behind her ear. 'You're welcome here *anytime*. You can just turn up whenever you need to. And I can let Simon know what's going on if you like, so you can come even if I'm at work.'

'It's really kind of you, but this would be the *first* place Justin would look for me. Plus Simon's not exactly a fan of kids, is he?'

Annie rolls her eyes. 'I know. He's of the *children should be seen and not heard* brigade.'

'And my kids aren't what you'd call children who are seen and not heard, are they?' I smile, suddenly missing them more than ever. I'll never get used to them spending each weekend with their dad.

'Couldn't you leave them with their dad for a few days and come here on your own?'

'If you lived somewhere that Justin wouldn't look for me, I'd consider it. But, if I'm honest, I don't really want to do that. If he and Cara get their claws into them for any length of time...' I shudder as my voice trails off. Amongst other things, Rick's new wife spoils them rotten in ways I can't afford to compete with. It's as if she's trying to win them over. One of these days, they're going to tell me they'd prefer to leave me and live with their dad and stepmum. And I'm feeling so low in myself at the moment that a part of me wouldn't even blame them.

'Blimey - can you hear him?'

We pause for a moment. Simon's elevated voice echoes through an open window. Then a loud bang, like a thunderclap, emanates from inside.

'What the hell's going on?'

An icy unease grips me as the sudden silence unsettles the air. I can't tell Annie that I've already got a *very* good idea of what could be going on in there.

Justin will be feeling pretty desperate now he's lost his job. When he initially broached his money-making plan with me, I convinced myself it was a joke. But I saw something in his eyes that told me if he was pushed far enough into a corner, he'd be more than capable of blackmailing one of the few friends he's got left in life. That's the only thing I can imagine going on in there right now.

I steal a quick look at Annie. All is well in her world as far as she knows, apart from the virus situation. I *don't* want to be the person responsible for shattering her marriage. We spent time as a four – them and us – before things began to go wrong between me and Justin. They seemed so happy together and she's shown me so much sympathy and friendship that I can't bear to hurt her. If Justin could have only kept what he knew to himself...

'You need to finish that tea and get yourself organised. I'll do my best to keep Justin here and give you some time – though that will depend on whatever's gone on between him and Simon.'

'How on earth will you manage that?' I wrap my fingers around the mug – its warmth is comforting.

'I'll just ply him with pints of beer, don't worry.' She grins.

'You're a goodun - I really appreciate you trying.' I get to my feet. An eerie silence has engulfed the place. I pray Justin hasn't slipped back out of the front door. If he has – *everything* could be scuppered.

'You'll keep me posted won't you?'

'Of course I will.'

'And if all else fails,' Annie calls after me. 'I'll swipe something nasty from our ward's medicine cabinet.'

'What for?'

'For you to slip into his food, of course.'

I smile back at her over my shoulder. Her voice might be filled with sweetness and light – but she'd be only too happy to do whatever it takes to set me free from Justin – if she could get away with it.

4

I slip through the back gate of the beer garden to make the short walk home. A stone's throw from The Old Crown, Justin clearly chose this house with the intention of also choosing his local pub when he first bought it with his ex-wife.

I had my reservations about moving into a house another woman had originally chosen but decided I'd be able to put my own stamp on things and make it a happier home than it had evidently been in the past.

Other than its proximity to the pub, it looked perfect when I first visited. With its ample gardens and lots of space inside, it was a far cry from the poky and dingy terraced house where the kids had even been forced to share a bedroom.

The new tenant mentioned by Annie doesn't seem to be wasting any time in getting herself moved into the vacant flat. As if she thought *we* could have taken it on – even some of its windows overlook ours. I need to get as far away as I can from Justin – somewhere he won't find us easily, especially now I'm carrying his baby.

If I were to track back to a turning point in his behaviour, I'd place it at around the time I discovered I was pregnant. Perhaps part of it is that he's scared of being a dad again – of losing another child like he's already lost Cameron. But whatever the reason behind it, it's not good enough.

Hopefully, by the time he manages to find me, he'll have already moved on to some other poor unsuspecting woman he can tell all his sob stories to. He'll have someone else to bully and leech from.

Justin, by his own admission, finds it impossible to be alone – the main reason, he said, why he wanted me to move in here as soon as he did. My gut was telling me to wait but when he got down on one knee in front of the garden gate, I couldn't help but be swept up in the romance of the whole thing. But I should have listened to my gut.

I linger at our gate now, fingertips feeling for the contours of the ring he bestowed upon me in this very spot. Then I remember where I put it – in a pot on the kitchen sink because my fingers are too swollen to wear my rings. Justin's even had a go at me for that, accusing me of not wanting to wear them so I can attract other men. *As if!*

The new woman also lingers at her gate to the three-floor block of flats. She shakes her hair behind one shoulder as she appears to fix her gaze on me. Evidently of a similar age, she might be considering whether to come over and introduce herself. Before she gets the chance, I close the gate behind me and head for the door around the back of the house. Not only can I not be bothered with small talk, the way I'm feeling, but I've already exposed myself to more than enough risk from other people's germs for one day.

If that virus ends up in Otley it's *not* going to find me.

I ignore the *yoohoo* of Diane from next-door-but-one. She eventually forgave me for telling her to mind her own business when I was moving in, but will still take any opportunity to continue to bombard me with her unsolicited advice. Since she cottoned on that I'm expecting, there seems to have been plenty more as well.

She and I have warmed to each other now but she doesn't even *try* to hide her dislike of Justin.

As I put my key in the lock, I glance in the opposite direction to where Diane's waving at me. *I haven't seen you. I haven't heard you.* My hair's over my ears so if she says anything at a later date, I'll pretend I had headphones in.

The playground at the centre of our square, usually teeming with preschoolers and young mums, is deserted today. My children's eyes were out on stalks when they first saw the swings and slides over there – it was a world away from the outside space we had in our former backyard. There wasn't enough room to swing a mouse out there, let alone a cat. My two were as excited as I was about moving in here to start with. It would have been nice to have become part of the community that exists around the square, but sadly, it isn't to be for us.

Every time I think of my kids, my chest feels as heavy as a submarine. Especially now it's become necessary to subject them to further upheaval. I've never dealt well with guilt.

Clicking the door behind me, I kick my sandals off and they land with a clatter on the wooden floor. Justin likes shoes off in the house. There's no sign of his shoes, however; there's no indication that Justin's been back here at all. Annie must be managing to keep him occupied at the pub. I head into the kitchen to throw open the patio doors while I get everything sorted. The sun moves to the back of the house on an afternoon so it gets like a sauna in here.

Justin could turn up at any moment so I need to be quick with it all. The chair creaks under me as I fire up my laptop and run my eyes down the list of emails. There's still nothing from the agent. Yet again, I check my call log, trying to quell the sense of unease that's expanding through my chest. Again, there's absolutely nothing. Annie was right – I can't just sit around waiting for the agent to contact me. Especially since I've heard for myself what sort of mood Justin's likely to be in when he returns. There's no guesswork required today.

I click on a new browser and search for Matthew and Co. Letting Agents. My heart is pulsing like a nightclub beat as I copy their number into my phone. *Why on earth didn't I just ring them this morning?* No way should I have left it this late.

As I'm about to hit call, the sudden ring of my phone makes me jump. It's Rick. What does *he* want? He wouldn't usually ring on a Monday. He doesn't usually call me *full stop*. Though it's tempting to ignore him and get on with what I'm supposed to be doing, my curiosity is piqued.

'It's me,' he announces.

'So I gather. What's up?'

'I just thought you should know, I've got the kids here.'

'At your house?' My voice rises. 'Since when?' I push my chair back with a scrape and stride over to the sink. 'They should still be at school.'

'School rang me just before lunch.' His voice bears a trace of smugness. 'To pick them up.'

'Why would they call *you?* I'm the first point of contact.' Perhaps there's something wrong with my phone. This could be the reason why the letting agent hasn't been able to reach me. And now school.

'Haven't you been watching the news, Melissa? They've shut all the schools.'

'Are you being serious?' I pace the floor, my bare feet slapping against the tiles. 'I know they were talking about it earlier, but—'

'Never mind all that.' He pauses. 'But you need to know that the kids *wanted* to come here.' I can hear the smile in his voice. He sounds even more smug now.

'Hang on.' I lift my eyes to the clock. 'It's after three. Why am I only just finding out about school being closed?'

'Because they rang *me*,' he repeats. 'Like I just said, the kids asked them to.'

'Why would they do that?' I close my eyes. I already know the answer and can only imagine the turmoil they must have felt in coming to this decision.

'Why do *you* think?' His tone seems to darken.

'But it's not your day Rick.' I'm not going to rise to his bait. I'll act normal and when I get them back, I'll speak to them properly. 'You've already had them all weekend. When are you bringing them home?'

'I'm not,' he replies.

'Pardon?' For a moment, I wonder if I've misheard him. Surely he wouldn't do this to me, he wouldn't *really* prevent the kids from returning to me.

'They don't want to be around *him*,' Rick goes on. 'And after what they've been telling me about your miserable home life, I don't want them around him either.'

Something inside me gives way and I sink back to my chair. I've always known this situation would arrive sooner or later. Aisla has started wetting the bed, which at the age of eight, she's hugely ashamed about. She's always been a real daddy's girl so I should've known she'd confide in Rick sooner or later about what's been going on here.

Then there's Ewan, only two years older than her, who's taken it upon himself to act as my protector, whether Justin's yelling at me, storming around the house, or worse. The fact that I'm expecting Ewan's little brother or sister probably adds to his need to defend me.

No matter how much I've tried to banish him to his room along with Aisla, he refuses to budge. And now he doesn't want to be here at all. It's so wrong – I should never have stayed this long. Which is why I'm getting out before they become any more affected.

I'm leaving Justin, no matter what. Then as soon as I'm out of here, I'll start the divorce proceedings. I'll be twice divorced before I'm even forty.

'I'm sorting it all out, Rick. I promise.' The words falter in my throat, a feeble attempt to reassure. The fragility of my promise hangs in the air, a desperate plea for understanding. My voice, though small, echoes around the quiet kitchen. I try to keep a neutral tone, masking the turbulence within me.

From the very first time Rick and Justin locked eyes, a palpable dislike hung in the air, thickening with each shared glance and exchanged word since. I've had to prevent Justin on several occasions from bad-mouthing Rick in front of the children. In addition to this, I've been forced to extend the children's stay at their dad's each weekend by another night.

After Justin tried to attack Rick in front of the children in January, he refuses to come anywhere near this house anymore. I have no choice other than to accept him dropping them off at school on a Monday morning instead of returning them on Sunday night like he used to. Every weekend, I ache for them, yet must always keep it under wraps for fear of upsetting Justin.

'How are you *sorting it*?' Rick's words drip with sarcasm. It would be so easy to lose it with him here, particularly given the way I'm feeling right now, but I need to keep things civil between us. It's not as if I'm in a very strong position at the moment.

Behind Rick's voice, I can hear a TV and the voices of my children. I'm heartbroken that they haven't wanted to come home to me – yet, at the same time, I completely understand. It's not as if it's *me* they don't want to come back to – it's a hundred per cent Justin. In the last few months since everything turned sour, I've let him have enough control over my life. I can't allow him to come between me and my children any more than he already has. The sooner I get out of here, the better.

'Can I speak to them please?'

I haven't seen Aisla and Ewan since Friday morning when I dropped them off at school. For many mums, the space from school uniforms, spelling tests and lunch boxes might be a relief, but for me, it's torture.

5

'Aisla's really upset.' Rick lowers his voice. 'She feels terrible at not wanting to come back to you, and as for Ewan, well he's worried sick about it all. It's just not on, Melissa.'

'I know it isn't.' My voice wobbles, choked with unspent tears. He's keeping my kids – this is really happening.

'A ten-year-old shouldn't be panicking about the safety of his mother,' he continues. 'Based on her own hasty and reckless decisions.'

'Am I to assume the school knows *everything* about our situation as well?'

'Is that all you care about?'

'Of course not. Look, Rick, you can't make me feel any worse than I already do. I'm trying—'

'In answer to your question, the school knows you're with a man who gets pissed, shouts at you and the kids, and thinks it's OK to punch holes in the walls in front of them.'

I glance up at the latest one from Thursday night. I can't even recall what provoked him. If I'm not careful, I'll end up with social services on the doorstep before too long. How can I tell Rick that each move I make feels like I'm walking a tightrope between the harsh reality of my crumbling life and my desire to protect the kids?

'As their father, I can't allow them to live with someone like that.'

I can hardly argue with him. 'I know.' I slump further to the table and stare out at the garden. Aisla's wellingtons are standing beside the shed and next to them is Ewan's bike, which he was supposed to have put away.

'The question is, Melissa.' Rick's voice softens. 'What are you doing about it?'

'I'm sorting it.'

'OK. I'm relieved to hear it. So long as you understand they'll have to stay with us until you do.'

'But, but – I don't know how long it's going to take me.' I look at the clock again. Time's ticking on and I need to get those keys today. But what if I can't? What if we lock down like Italy and—

'They're staying with us until you're away from *him*. I mean it.'

'But please – what if we – look, please don't do this to me.' The magnitude of what's going on here is really sinking in.

'I can't just let them come back and be around that man, Melissa. Not after what they've told their teachers today. And Cara agrees with me.'

A vision of Rick's new wife enters my mind. She'll be lapping all this up, no doubt. I know from the kids that she and Rick want a baby of their own and until this happens for them, *my* children seem to fill that space for her. I know I should be relieved that she makes Aisla and Ewan feel more than welcome in her home and wanted while they're staying there, and I *am* grateful. However, the maternal part of me, the part I can't seem to control, feels incredibly pushed out and well, jealous. The woman helped herself to my husband when we were still together, and now it feels like she's trying to steal my children from me. And right now, I haven't got a leg to stand on.

His betrayal with Cara almost destroyed me - and was even more of a kick in the teeth as it echoed exactly what my dad did to my mum when I was the same age as Aisla.

Then when he had more kids with his new wife, I became even more pushed out. Aisla and Ewan are *everything* to me, and Rick and Cara are *not* keeping hold of them – missing them at weekends is unbearable enough as it is without the possibility of this continuing indefinitely.

'I'm leaving him – really I am.' I close my eyes. The enormity of what I'm revealing to Rick, the second person I've trusted with this information, sinks in. Will he use my instability against me?

'When will that be then?' We're back to his sarcastic tone of voice.

'It could be today, or it could be tomorrow, but it'll be as soon possible. I'm just waiting to get the keys from the letting agent.'

'The keys to where, exactly?'

'A house I've found near the kids' school.' Really, I need to get off this phone and do what I need to do. Especially now.

'You're moving them *again*? It's little wonder Aisla's so unsettled.'

'God, I can't win here, can I?' I drop my head into my hands. 'You don't want them to be around Justin, but even when I'm telling you I'm leaving, you're—'

'So they'll have a third home to settle into?' he cuts in. 'Actually, a fourth home if you include our place, in just over a year.'

'Do I need to remind you who blew our family apart in the first place?' I snap, thankfully finding my kick-ass side at last. This is a complete nightmare. Justin could walk through this door at any moment, and here I am, arguing with my ex-husband over the kids. 'You can't just *take* them from me Rick – not like this. They live with *me.*'

'I'm not *just taking them*. You can have them back when you've got yourself completely away from that waste of space, and secured somewhere safe for them to live,' he replies. 'I mean it Melissa –

them being forced to live in the sort of environment you've been offering is harming them.'

A fat tear plops from my chin onto the table. I can't hold the tears back any longer. 'I was just about to ring the letting agent when you called me,' I begin, no longer able to keep the sorrow from my voice. 'I'm going to get off the phone now Rick. I'll let you know when I've got it all sorted.'

'OK.' His voice softens again. He's never been able to bear me crying, even when we were splitting up. 'And whether you believe me or not, Melissa, I really *am* sorry it's come to this.'

'So am I,' I reply. But he's already gone.

I inhale deeply, trying to steady the quiver in my chest. My rapid breaths are doing a rhythmic dance with the chaos swirling around me. The keys to that house are our lifeline, our ticket to a new beginning. I hit the call button on the number for the agent. Getting my hands on those keys this afternoon has now tripled in urgency. I just want my kids back. I *need* them back.

This is Matthew and Co, Letting Agents. Due to the continued uncertainty and the potential of upcoming Government action due to the Coronavirus pandemic, our offices are temporarily closed. This mailbox and our email inbox will be monitored, so please leave a message and we will get back to you as soon as possible.

Frustration boils within me. 'This bloody virus!' I mutter, unable to comprehend its relentless impact. First my work, then the school – now everything's being affected.

'This is Melissa Rose,' I blurt. 'I paid a holding fee for a house I looked at last week and you said I could have the keys when the current tenant hands them in.' I'm gabbling but I need to get all this said in case there's a message time limit. 'I need the keys – I need them today - I've got the deposit and a month's rent all ready for you. Please call me back – it's really urgent.'

I open my email to search for the message I got from the man who showed me around. My vision blurs with tears, distorting the screen and the looming uncertainty before me. I'm crying all the time at the moment – I think it's part hormones and part circumstances. Justin's repeatedly told me I'm unbearable to be around. This, he says, is why he spends so much of his time in the pub.

I fire off an email saying something similar to my voicemail. Surely they'll check their messages before the end of the afternoon? *They've got to.*

The house we're supposed to be moving into is even pokier than the one we left last year, but it will have to do for now. As soon as I can get back to work, I'll ask for extra hours. Then I'll save up for somewhere better – I'll get a second job for as long as I'm still able to work, until the baby comes along. I'll do whatever it takes.

Still, it won't hurt to keep looking – perhaps something else could be immediately available for us. The way things are turning out, I'd be tempted to accept somewhere without even viewing it first.

I type, *houses to rent in Otley.* Most of the houses the search returns are already let by Matthew and Co., with *let agreed* banners across them. But there are a few other places with another local estate agent, including one I could go for straight away. It's *mostly furnished,* which would be helpful since I won't be able to take much from here. It's an extra couple of hundred pounds to afford the first month's rent, but I can scrape that together. I open another browser to log into my bank account. I should just about have enough, but I need to double-check before ringing to see if the house is still available. If not, I'll apply for an overdraft.

I let a long breath out. I've got enough. And the house is only on the other side of Otley. If I can just manage to get someone from the agency to meet me there within the next couple of hours, they might let me have the keys straight away. My fingers fumble, desperately pressing the buttons on my phone. Within seconds I'm connected to a recorded message – and it's a similar one to before.

'Bloody hell!' I slam my phone onto the table.

Just as the front door bangs.

6

Justin bursts into the kitchen, his footsteps resonating with an agitated energy. I slam the lid on my laptop before sliding my phone back towards me across the table and dropping it into my handbag.

Over an hour has passed since I left Annie in the beer garden. I expected Justin to drown his sorrows more than he seems to have done. His sobriety raises more questions than answers.

'I've been fired,' he announces, banging his flask onto the counter.

Spare me the obvious, I almost retort. Clearly, he never realised I was outside with Annie when he arrived at the pub earlier. He was, no doubt, too busy giving ultimatums to his so-called friend.

'Why?' I need to act normal here. If he gets even the slightest sniff of what I'm up to, he'll be banging more than his flask onto the counter.

'So he doesn't have to pay me anything if this virus shit gets any worse. He's taken the tools I was using – everything.' He turns his back to me and grips the edge of the sink.

I stare at his hunched shoulders. 'I don't know what to say.' It's true – I don't.

'Now *that* pillock's barred me from the pub as well.' He lets go of the sink and marches over to the fridge. 'What a brilliant day I'm having.'

'Who? Simon? What do you mean, *barred you?*' I remain sitting at the table. Perhaps it would be better to get well out of the way, while I'm so unsure about Justin's mood. I can't take any more today.

'I've just been walking around.' He wrenches a beer from the shelf. 'Trying to get my head back together before I do him some damage.'

'Why's he barred you?' I'll ignore the part about him *doing him some damage.* I've got more than enough to worry about as it is.

'Why do you think?'

'You went through with your plan, I take it.' I hardly dare look at his face. Instead, I stare down at his work boots, resisting the urge to ask why the rest of us have to leave our shoes at the door.

'I certainly did.' He puffs his chest out. 'I've definitely left him with food for thought, let's put it that way.'

'But he's supposed to be your friend, I honestly thought you were joking when you—'

'Five grand's nothing to him.'

'Five grand? Oh my God. What are you playing at?'

Simon must rue the day he attended that stag party in January more than any other regret in his life.

'What choice did I have? I've lost my job; at least, it'll keep me afloat for a while.'

He makes it sound like he's applied for a bank loan.

'It's outright blackmail, Justin. He could involve the police.'

I could even be implicated. After all, I knew what Justin was planning, but I didn't take him completely seriously.

'Aren't you bothered about what he's done to your friend? I thought the two of you were as thick as thieves. Don't you think a man who can't keep it in his trousers should get what's coming to him?'

'Yes, I do – which is why Annie should be told. But *this*—'

'I'd never be unfaithful to you, you know.' He cracks his can of beer open with a hiss. Judging by the tone of his voice, he's just said something he thinks I should be grateful for.

No, but you'd do lots of other things besides. Instead of saying this, I try to settle my voice. 'You must see this is all wrong, Justin. Blackmailing your friend over a one-night stand - and I still can't think why you ever told *me* about it. I didn't need to know and I certainly never wanted to.'

'I wish I hadn't. But I was drunk,' he replies. 'Anyway – it was more than *one* night – didn't I tell you?' He spins around to face me. 'We were away for *two* nights. I'm sure I told you about him going back for more and...' A grin spreads across his face. I used to love his smile. Now I'd love to have the guts to slap it away. 'I've got video evidence to prove it.'

I stare at him. I thought he was such a good-looking man until I realised how ugly he can be inside. 'You do realise I'm going to *have* to tell Annie,' I say. 'One night's unforgivable enough but *two*? She's got a right to know.'

'Like I've already said...' His expression hardens. 'You can't say a thing – what leverage will I have with Simon if you do? You'll ruin everything.'

'I don't care about any of that.' I try to fill my voice with an authority I'm not feeling. 'What you're doing is wrong.'

'When I want you to sit in your high and mighty judgement of me, I'll ask you, alright?'

At least we're having what could probably be construed as a *normal* argument – at least, by our standards. Luckily, as things stand, he appears to have zero idea about what I'm planning to do. Part of me would love to witness his reaction when he realises I've had the guts to leave him, but the other part of me never wants to think or feel anything about him ever again, once I've managed to get myself and the kids away.

'Look, can we just leave all this alone for now Justin – I honestly wish you'd never told me about any of it – it's got *nothing* to even do with me.' I do need to get away from him – the letting agent could have messaged me by now and once he does, there won't be a second to spare.

'I need to be sure you're not going to get involved.' He steps closer to me. 'Judging from the way you're acting, I'm not sure I can trust you.'

'I'm not going to say a word.'

Yet.

'You repeat a thing and I'll tell her it was *you* he's been sleeping with.'

'What?' His words take a moment to sink in. I should have known he'd be capable of acting out such a ridiculous threat. He's pretty much capable of anything. There seems to be few depths the man won't plummet to.

'Don't be so ridiculous – why would you lie like that? What on earth's got into you?'

'I'll say I found the two of you together,' he continues. 'And that's just for starters. Don't push me on this Melissa – I need that money, especially now.'

'I've just said I'm not going to say a word.' My voice rises as I repeat myself. He's locked into himself again and is clearly not listening to me.

Even if he were to lie, as he's threatening to, Annie wouldn't believe him in a million years – no matter how plausible he can be when he puts his mind to it.

But she'll find out what Simon did sooner or later, whether it ends up being Justin who spills the beans, or me. It's such a shame that he's done what he's done. I thought they were happy together – they only got married just after we did.

'And what if I don't believe you?' There's the hint of a threat in his voice. I'm so sick of living like this.

I don't think Justin would ever hit me, especially now that I'm pregnant, but he's pinned me to enough walls and floors to suspect that he'll do more to me than try to *turn the tables* when I let Annie know what Simon got up to behind her back.

But as soon as I've escaped from this marriage and left here, I'll be safe to tell her. Now I know it wasn't just a drunken one-off and that he went back to the woman for more, there's no way I can justify not telling her.

But right now, I need to focus on getting away from Justin. I have to sort out what I'm going to do before it's too late. Perhaps I'll tell him that I'm going for a walk. However, he'll watch to see if I'm taking my phone. That's how he operates. He'll get suspicious and might even say he's coming with me. I look up at him, and I'm even more unsettled when I notice how intently he's watching me.

7

MY MUM often used to say that my facial expressions always belied what I'm thinking. Judging by how Justin's standing, well towering, right in front of me, I really hope he can't read how I'm plotting my escape.

We stare at each other for a moment. We're like opponents in a ring more than the happily married couple we tried to be. It's unfathomable to me now how I ever ended up marrying and expecting my third child with this man. I guess at the time, I thought I had him sussed out. All I could see was a happy future for us.

After becoming more and more estranged from his son, he said that all he ever wanted was a family to fill these four walls with love and laughter again. However, as things have turned out, they've been filled with anything but.

'I hope you're not planning to double-cross me on this, Melissa.'

'I'm not.' My voice rises. He's not going to let up.

'As my wife, your loyalty should be with *me*.'

What can I say to that? 'Look, Justin. Can we just change the subject? I was thinking I might go for a walk. It's a lovely day, and—'

'You've only known the woman for five minutes.' He's like a dog with a bone. 'And in any case,' he continues, 'I reckon you only made friends with her to keep tabs on me in the pub.'

The former me would inform him that he shouldn't flatter himself, but that's only going to allow this conversation to drag on. I raise my bag to my shoulder and head towards the hallway. He hasn't challenged what I said about going for a walk so maybe I can just slip out. I need to work out what the hell I'm going to do to get my kids back with me.

'What are you doing at home at this time anyway?' He calls after me.

I turn in the doorway. 'Work sent me home this morning. Until further notice.'

'Why?' He drinks deeply from his can. 'Because of this so-called virus? It's complete crap if you ask me. Media scaremongering.' He appears in the doorway of the kitchen.

'Is it complete crap though? We don't know that.' Oh bloody hell, I've unwittingly entered into another conversation with him. I don't know why I'm wasting my breath. Any opinion that differs from Justin's is always invalid.

'You're obviously one of the people who believe all the scaremongering.'

'I think it's more than that. Anyway, like I said, I'm going for a walk.' I sit on the bottom step to fasten my sandals. My baby bump, while still small, hinders me from reaching my feet. It's a gentle reminder of the life growing within me.

'Just hang on will you? We need to talk.' He comes towards me.

'I thought we had.' I could scream. A sense of frustration hangs over me as the impossibility of escaping him settles in.

'Like I said, I've been fired.' At least he's changed the subject from Annie and Simon. 'And you've been sent home from work. So what the hell are we meant to live on?'

Little does he know that he'll be fending for himself in the not-too-distant future. 'I've got some holiday pay to come,' I reply. 'But to be honest, I don't know. Work didn't say anything about how long we'll be off or whether we'll even be paid.'

This is a nightmare. I might have the money to leave him, but what we'll live on beyond that is anyone's guess. I just have to keep the faith that something will turn up – it usually does.

After I've disentangled myself from him, I'm staying single. All I want to do is immerse myself in being the best mum to my soon-to-be three kids. Then I'll get back to work and see what I can do about climbing the ladder at the hotel. I'm going to make something of myself – I really am. Never again will I find myself in this sort of position.

I rise from the step and find myself facing him. 'If I can just get past,' I say, as though I'm speaking to a stranger instead of my husband.

'Not so fast.' He checks his watch. 'Aren't you supposed to have picked the kids up from school by now?'

Damn! Why didn't I use this as an excuse in the first place?

'Why did you say you're going for a walk?' He takes my chin in his hands and tilts my face towards his. 'What's going on, Melissa?'

I look away from him and study the pattern on the wallpaper we chose together. 'They've been sent home as well.'

'So where are they then?' He takes a long drink from his beer while looking around him as though they're suddenly going to appear. *I wish.*

'They're actually at Rick's.' I wonder if he can sense the heaviness in my words. I can hardly believe Rick's calling all the shots with them. What the hell has my life come to?

Justin looks confused for a moment then surveys me with his steely-grey eyes as he tilts his head to one side. 'I thought you got them back on a Monday.'

Think, think, think. 'It's this Covid thing. You know, with my asthma and with me being pregnant. They're with Rick as a precaution.' I'm stuttering away here but I can hardly tell him the real reason they're at their dad's house.

'What are you on about?' He drains his can and scrunches it within his hand.

'If one of the kids brings the virus home from school and I catch it – well I'm technically more at risk than other people, aren't I?'

He frowns slightly, his face is now a cross between being pleased and being suspicious. 'So how long are they staying with their dad for?'

'I don't know. ' My phone bursts into life from inside my handbag and something inside my chest lurches – a combination of nerves and excitement.

'Hang on a sec – I need to take this.' Avoiding his eye, I turn on my heel and rush up the stairs. 'It's probably to do with the kids.'

8

_____

I DON'T RECOGNISE the number so it *must* be the letting agent – I can't think who else it could be.

'Hi there – this is Jonathan from Matthew and Co. I've just received your message.'

It is!

'I'd hoped you might have called me earlier.' I sink to the edge of the bed, slightly out of breath from running up the stairs. As yet, Justin doesn't appear to have come after me which is a relief. He's probably busy getting some more beer down his neck.

'I can only apologise. You know how it is with all that's going on right now.'

I might as well get straight to the point. 'Can I still have the keys to the house today?' I cross my fingers in the mirrored wardrobe facing me. Once I've got the keys, I've then just got to find the opportunity to get out of here which, admittedly, will be easier while Aisla and Ewan are with Rick. I've already got lots of our stuff packed - all I'll need is to somehow get Justin out of the way for two or three hours. Hopefully, he'll find a new pub to turn into his second home, now he's been barred from The Old Crown.

The agent's momentary hesitation tells me all I need to know.

Then the tone of his voice confirms my fears. 'I'm so sorry,' he begins, 'but the current tenants are having to stay there for the time being. I literally only found out half an hour ago.' To his credit, he does sound genuinely apologetic. But this doesn't help me right now. I feel like beating my fists into the pillows. I don't want to stay here a moment longer – I *can't* stay here. What about my kids?

'But – but they said they were leaving, didn't they?' My anger has quickly given way to hopelessness and I'm struggling not to cry again.

He seems to sense this with the note of sympathy I detect in his voice. 'Apparently, things have been put on hold for them. With where they were going, I mean. The new job one of them was supposed to be starting has been postponed as well.'

'But you promised me the keys today.' I stand from the bed, clutching a fistful of my fringe as I start pacing up and down in front of the mirror. The fabric of my dress is really showing off my baby bump today and I'm at a stage where it's obvious I'm expecting. With my other two, I was never happier than at this point in both pregnancies – over the sickness and starting to bloom. But this time around, I've never felt more miserable.

'And you can still have them. The property's still yours, of course. Just as soon as the current tenants can move out.'

'Did they say when that'll be?'

'I guess they can't at the moment. Until the powers that be get on top of this virus thing, we're all in limbo, I'm afraid.' A dog barks in his background and a door bangs. He must have received my email and be ringing me from home. I bet his home life is *nothing* like mine. He won't have to walk on eggshells and be at the mercy of his partner's mood and drinking, never knowing what each day is going to bring.

I throw myself back onto the bed. *What am I going to do?*

'Have you got any other properties that are empty at the moment?' Having now checked, I know I've got a couple of hundred pounds more than I budgeted for, so can stretch myself slightly if need be. 'I am rather desperate.'

'I really *am* sorry. We don't have anything right now. But as soon as—'

'What are you doing up there Melissa?' Justin's voice echoes from the bottom of the stairs. 'Who are you talking to?'

Bloody hell. He's on his way up. 'I've got to go,' I whisper urgently into the phone. 'Please call as soon as you have the keys back.'

'Who've you been on the phone to?' Justin's standing in the doorway, cracking open his second can of beer. If he keeps on like this, it won't be long before he'll go to bed for an hour or two to sleep it off. It's always the case when he drinks in the daytime.

'Oh, it was only Rick.' I try to keep my voice as nonchalant as I can. 'It was just a quick call.'

'So why run off with your phone like that?'

'Well, it's just that you don't like each other, do you? I didn't think you'd want to listen to me talking to him.' Here I go again, trying to appease him. It's all I seem to have done lately.

'Are you sure that's all it is?' He leans against the doorframe. 'You wouldn't be trying to pull the wool over my eyes, would you?'

'Of course not.' I lock eyes with him, my gaze unwavering. The room feels heavy with the weight of my hatred – a visceral emotion that swirls in the air, a silent battleground between me and this man who's inserted himself between me and my kids, attempting to assert control over every aspect of my life.

Breaking our eye contact, I look down at my arms which are covered in grab-shaped bruises from last week. I'm surprised he hasn't said anything about me wearing this sleeveless dress which puts them on show.

'Rick doesn't *normally* ring you – I thought he avoided it at all costs.' His words are laced with suspicion.

'He was letting me know the kids are OK, that's all.' I trace the pattern on the duvet with my finger. The room, with its ensuite bathroom and fitted furnishings, feels like both a sanctuary and a prison. I won't miss *him*, but part of me will miss this room.

'Why wouldn't they be OK?' He narrows his eyes.

'You know, just with them being out of their usual routine and all that.' I'm struggling to keep this air of cheeriness in my voice so he doesn't suspect what's really going on. At best, he might try to get involved and at worst, he'll know which way I'm going to go, in terms of Rick's ultimatum and will be watching me like a hawk.

Really, I'm gutted, absolutely gutted, that I've got no way of getting Aisla and Ewan back with me today – or possibly even within the next few days with how things are looking. But the minute I can get some breathing space from Justin, I'm not going to stop ringing around letting agents and landlords until I find somewhere for us to go. *Anywhere.*

Justin steps further into the room, his presence carrying the faint scent of stale alcohol which is clinging to his work clothes. The acrid aroma fills the space, a silent reminder of the tension that lingers between us. He places his can on the chest of drawers, the metallic click echoing in the charged atmosphere.

'Anyway,' I spring up from the bed. 'I might as well get a few jobs done around the house. I'm feeling a bit lost without the kids here, to be honest.' I try to edge my way around him but he steps to the side, blocking me.

'If you're at a loose end.' He nods toward the bed, his eyes crinkling in the corners as he smirks at me. 'We've no kids, have we? Or work? I can think of worse ways to pass an hour.'

I can't think of anything more dreadful. 'I'm sorry,' I reply in the most pained voice I can muster. 'I'm still feeling a bit sickly.' I pat my stomach.

'I thought you were over all that now.'

'It's not as bad as it was, but it still comes and goes.'

I can tell by his face that he doesn't believe me. 'I'll take your mind off it then.'

'I'm going to do a few bits in the garden. I need some fresh air.' Miraculously, he allows me to slither around the side of him and out of the door towards the top of the stairs.

'You chill out and drink your beer,' I call back. If I sound patronising, I don't care. It's all he ever does when he's at home. Drink.

I brace myself for some nasty comment about being *frigid* or *boring* to follow me, as it often does when I reject him in this way.

9

JUSTIN'S RESPONSE is a stoic silence. What he doesn't know is that my pregnancy sickness completely subsided a couple of weeks ago. In fact, other than my rapidly tightening waistbands, I barely feel any different than I did before.

I panicked when I first discovered I was expecting, especially since I'd already made the decision, not long after Christmas, that I was going to leave him. Being a single mother of two children is challenging enough. So how would I cope on my own with a newborn baby? Since that initial panic, I've had the chance to get my head around everything and have convinced myself that I'll be OK. Thankfully, I've grown just as attached to this baby as I was to Aisla and Ewan when I was carrying them. I'm now longing for the reassurance of this baby's first movements inside me. I know from experience these could be any time soon.

'Should you be carrying that?' Justin raises an eyebrow as he jogs back down the stairs. A touch of concern laces his voice.

'It's only a washing basket – I'll be fine.' If only he could have been this considerate all the time, then I wouldn't be facing all this upheaval. But the nice side of him only comes out in fits and starts these days, and we never know what we're going to get in between.

I close the side door behind me. The unseasonable heat slaps me in the face as I step into the sunshine. Normally, unexpected weather such as this would lift my mood, no matter what's going on. The way things are looking for me, however, I doubt even a crane could lift it.

I stripped the kids' beds this morning and washed their sheets – all ready for our so-called move. The current occupants have said they're taking their washing machine with them when they move out, so I won't have one. I truly believed I'd be pegging this stuff out in the backyard of our new rented terrace, instead of here.

Tears fill my eyes as I fasten firstly Aisla's Barbie pillowcase, and then Ewan's football pillowcase to the washing line. As if everything's come to this. Perhaps I should just turn up at Rick's and demand them back – no matter how much of a scene it might cause.

But the more logical side of me is only too aware that the children have had enough of being here. No matter how suitable the house or the surrounding area might be, they don't deserve to be around a stepfather who's affecting them so deeply with his foul moods and unpredictability. No, I'll get myself out first and then Rick cannot argue about me collecting the children.

Despite the late Monday afternoon hour, an unusual hush blankets the square. The long shadows cast by the sun stretch across the garden path, creating a tranquil but eerily quiet atmosphere. I'm used to the shrieks and shouts of children on the playground, and the hum of lawnmowers and strimmers from everyone's gardens. People are either hiding in their houses or are in front of their TVs, glued to the news. There's nothing else in the media apart from the virus. I've been trying to avoid it and just to stay in touch with the headlines. My levels of anxiety are through the roof enough as it is.

The peace is broken by the metallic crack of a beer can, followed by Justin's voice, carrying the weight of his anger, as it seeps through the open patio door.

I pause what I'm doing and try to listen. It sounds like he's arguing with someone on the phone. It's impossible to make out what he's saying, or even who he could be talking to, as his voice seems to drift further away from the kitchen. He must have moved to another room.

'How are you doing, Melissa?' Diane startles me as she calls in her sing-song voice from two doors away. Justin's planted some conifers around our garden for more privacy, but it'll be a few more years before they'll bring any. I'll be long gone. 'It's awful – all this stuff on the news, isn't it?'

'I've been sent home from work because of it,' I call back.

'Is that because of the baby? I did hear something about pregnant women needing to shield.'

'Apparently so.'

'Well, you make sure you're looking after yourself. And if you need anything, just shout.'

'I will. Thank you. Anyway, I'd better be getting on.'

I finish hanging the washing out and then sink to the garden wall next to the shed. I tug my phone from the pocket of my pinafore dress. I'll be able to continue wearing this as my belly grows, which I'm pleased about. It was Aisla who told Diane about the baby. *My mum's got my sister in her tummy,* she announced, when we bumped into her at the swings. Aisla's convinced she'll get a sister but Ewan *only* wants a brother.

Nostalgia sweeps over me, and I find myself fighting the longing for the man Justin once was – the man I thought I could build a future with. The stark reality is a bitter pill to swallow. I'm constantly racking my brain over what could have gone wrong. Things I could have perhaps done that might be to blame. However, I come up short every time. It's not me, it's *him*.

What I do know is that I urgently need to find somewhere for us to move into. I've looked at all the local agents so it's time to look further afield. I head onto a different agent's website and cast my search from a five to a twenty-mile radius, then I select a minimum of two bedrooms and hit search.

Several decent-looking houses pop up. I choose *book a viewing* on the first one and fill in the contact page. But filling out contact forms is no good. I need to find something *today*. I look up the number of the agent and hit call. But within a few seconds, I can tell from the answering message that it's the same old story. *Bloody coronavirus.* Even if all these houses are standing empty, there doesn't seem to be anyone around to arrange anything for me.

Meanwhile, back in the house, I can't hear Justin's voice so he must have finished his phone call.

I sigh deeply. If all this had happened two or three years ago, I could have stayed with Mum. Instead, her house has been sold off to finance her care. A vision of her face *before* she became a shell of her former self emerges in my mind. I miss her so much and would give anything right now to be able to go to her for help.

I fill in another couple of contact forms for potential houses before clicking into 'Apple News' to see what the latest is.

Announcement expected at 8:30 pm, all the headlines scream. A cold hand of fear grips me as I scan down the reports. Every one of them is saying that we're likely to follow Italy, Spain and France into a lockdown, where we won't even be *allowed* to leave our houses. This is insane – I can't believe what's going on.

Justin's eyes gleam as he bursts into the garden. 'Have you heard what's bloody happening?' His excitement feels out of place and sends a chill down my spine. And he's opening yet another can.

'How many of those are you drinking today?' I nod towards it. He's showing no signs of needing to sleep anything off. It's more likely, that he'll keep drinking and become either overbearingly needy or if I say the slightest thing out of turn, aggressive.

'Never you mind.' He frowns at me. 'You're only jealous because *you* can't have one. Anyway, since Simon's barred me from the pub, I've got to get a drink from *somewhere.*'

'Is that who you were on the phone to? I could hear you from out here.'

'I wasn't talking that loudly, was I?'

'You were practically shouting. See, it's like I said the other day - you don't even realise when you're doing it.'

He looks slightly sheepish, which is a turn-up for the books. 'What are you doing out here anyway? I thought you were just hanging the washing out.'

'Enjoying the sunshine – I'm making the most of it while it's here.'

'I see Simon's got himself a tenant for his old flat.' He nods to where the woman's leaning into the boot of her car. 'Like I told you – he's quids in. Yet he's dragging his feet more than I thought he would over the five grand I've asked him for.'

'No matter what he's done to Annie, I still think what you're doing is wrong.'

'When I want your opinion, Melissa, I'll ask for it.' As he says this, he doesn't take his eyes off the woman who's lugging a box from her car to the bottom door of the block of flats. It's as if she can sense our eyes boring into the back of her head for she suddenly swings around to face us.

She pauses in the same way as when I first arrived back home earlier. If she wanted something, why wouldn't she just shout over? Or come across? Perhaps it's because of this virus stuff. Everyone's keeping well away from other people. It's awful really.

I glance at Justin who's still staring straight back at her. 'Do you know her?' I look from him back to her, frowning.

'Let's go inside,' he says, without replying. 'I need to talk to you about something.'

10

'You left your computer logged in before.' Justin's voice is soft, and I'm getting a sense that his words are an observation rather than an accusation.

He leans against the kitchen counter, a can of beer in one hand and his thumb hooked into his belt loop with the other. Justin's face bears the rugged traces of neglect — days-old stubble clings to his jaw, his unkempt hair begs for a scissors' mercy, and the wrinkles in his clothes tell of a man indifferent to his appearance. When I first met him, he had a swagger about him that was more than compelling, and he treated me as though I was a queen. He was a far cry from the man who stands before me now.

'Did I?' I search his face, desperately seeking any clue to the storm brewing within him. My heart races and anxiety tightens its grip as I await his response. I also search my memory for what exactly I might have left on the screen. I was looking at all sorts of things before he came home. *Did I close all the pages down?* I definitely didn't erase my history. What an idiot I am. Yes, I'm hormonal at the moment and the girls at work have been jokingly calling me *baby brain,* but what a stupid, *stupid* mistake to have made. Especially when I've come as far as I have already. I was practically home and dry without this stupid virus dominating everything like it's doing.

'You never answered my question.' I'll try to distract him. 'About whether you and that new neighbour know each other.'

'I owe the woman some money, that's all,' he mutters, avoiding eye contact.

'What for?'

'For a job.'

'She did a job *for you?*'

'No, I was supposed to do a job for *her*. But I didn't.' He looks uncomfortable. 'Anyway, never mind changing the subject, Melissa.' His voice hardens. 'I saw your bloody email.' His words land between us like a grenade.

'What email?' Shit. Shit. *Shit!* I head to the sink to fill a glass with water. My hands are shaking but I need to keep busy while he's speaking to me – there is no way I can look at him.

'You know *exactly* what I'm talking about.'

I don't like his emphasis on the word *exactly*. Any minute now, he's going to erupt. Either that or I'll get his heartfelt promises of change. I gulp at the water. He clearly means the email to the letting agent. The one where I talked about being so desperate to move. Oh. My. God. If his mood goes the wrong way, I could be done for here.

I slowly raise my eyes from the sink to his face. I'm relieved to see that he looks more hurt and disappointed than angry. This is weird – I would have predicted for him to completely blow his top. To burst out into the garden ranting, or even onto the village green, proclaiming how all women should be burned at the stake. However, there's none of that. Perhaps he hasn't drunk enough.

'I'm sorry.' *Am I?* Sorry I ever met him perhaps. Sorry for trusting him. Sorry for inflicting him onto my poor kids. But am I sorry that I'm trying to leave him? Not in the slightest. I'm only sorry that he's managed to find out about it.

'So when were you planning to tell me?' He takes a long swig from his can and crunches it between his fist. Another one bites the dust.

I shrug. I don't know what I can say in reply. This is horrendous. For the first time today, I'm actually relieved the kids are with Rick.

Annie's words suddenly come swimming back to me, *the most dangerous time is when you're trying to leave.* She heard them when she had to do some awareness training around domestic abuse at work. Somehow I've got to turn this around. If he suddenly flips, I still have this little one inside me to protect.

'Why, Melissa?'

He loads a whole load of anguish into the word *why* and has an expression on his face that reminds me of a wounded animal. I can't believe he's even having to ask *why.*

I pull a chair from beneath the table. If I tuck myself safely under it, I'll be less exposed to him, especially my belly, and therefore harder to attack.

'I didn't want to leave – really I didn't.' I gabble away in an attempt to appease him. 'It was only after Christmas Day that I thought it would be the best thing all round.'

'So you've been planning to leave me since *Christmas?*'

'Off and on. Look, Justin, I never wanted it to come to this, but you were bloody awful to me. More importantly, you were cruel to my kids.'

'My kids. My kids! They're all you ever go on about.' His voice cracks with possessiveness, a dark undertone slicing through the air, a stark reminder of the toxic grip he holds on our lives. He reaches up and slides a bottle of whiskey from the top of the fridge. 'Wasn't I ever important to you too?'

He's said that last sentence in the past tense which could be a very good sign. Perhaps he's already begun to accept that I'm going to leave him.

11

AT LEAST AN HOUR'S passed since he'll have seen that email on my computer. This will have given him some time to get his head around what he's read.

The fact that he's also going onto the whiskey will have one of two outcomes. Either he'll numb himself more quickly into a drunken stupor and need to go to bed, or the stronger liquor will add fuel to his anger. The signs are good so far, and from what I can ascertain, it's going to go the way of the stupor.

'Of course *you* were important too,' I begin, also speaking in the past tense. 'But you have to admit, Justin, things have gone horribly wrong for us since Christmas.' What I really mean here is it was only when we got to Christmas that I saw his true colours and accepted what a mistake I'd made.

'It wasn't my fault I got locked up all night on Christmas Eve.'

'So whose fault was it then?'

'*Hers.* Bloody Lynette's.' He jerks his thumb in the direction of the front door as though she could be standing there. 'It's *her* fault Cameron won't speak to me. I was never going to have a decent Christmas after he told me where to go like he did. It's completely *her* fault I got pissed and got caught behind the wheel.'

This is Justin all over. He'll *never* take responsibility for anything he's done. 'None of that excuses how you treated me on Christmas Day. How you ruined things for all of us.'

I'll never forget how Aisla and Ewan were clutching each other as Justin hurled the meal I'd spent many hours preparing against the wall. Then he yanked a four-pack from the fridge and stormed out into the night. Before he came back, I rang Rick to ask him to take the children out of the way. I didn't know what else to do.

'I apologised for all that, didn't I? *Straight away.* And I meant it – I really did.' He bangs a glass onto the worktop and sloshes whiskey into it. Gone are the days, it seems, of him diluting spirits with cola. He's going to be wrecked if he carries on.

I want to tell him that I'd already decided to leave him by then – no apology would be enough for how he'd behaved. I just needed to save the money up. But I can't deny that my positive pregnancy test didn't cause me to wobble from my decision. Particularly when Justin began being extra nice in the new year. This is the thing with him – he's so Jekyll and Hyde – the problem is that I never know which version of him I'm going to get.

'You might have apologised for Christmas Day, but what about all the other stuff?'

He takes a swig of his whiskey and then wipes his mouth on the back of his hand. 'What other stuff?'

He seems to be in a receptive mood so I might as well take the opportunity to give him some harsh reminders. Perhaps, he'll be less likely to come after me when I manage to get out of here.

'You know – being drunk all the time, yelling at me and the kids, punching holes in walls, following me around, accusing me of things – I can't live like this – but more importantly, neither can my children.'

His face darkens and I wonder if I've said too much. He seems jealous to high heaven of the love and attention I have for Aisla and Ewan. Perhaps he'd be even worse with a new baby, given the time they take up. My reminders of his previous behaviours might only serve to wind him up. Especially now he's started drinking the hard stuff.

He tugs the chair out, faces me and sits. This is a positive move as often, he prefers to tower over me when we're disagreeing. At least we're on a level now. 'What if I said I wanted to change?' he says. Even something in his jaw has softened.

Yep – I'm going to get the *promises of change* version of him this evening. He's going to start begging me not to leave him any time at all. Until he's finally had enough to drink and goes to bed – I'll have no chance of escaping him.

'You've said you're going to change *before*, Justin.' It's all I can do not to roll my eyes at him. 'I honestly can't take all this upset. I should be looking after myself now, and not be stressed out because of you all the time.'

'I'm sorry Melissa – I really am.' His eyes betray a fleeting glimpse of remorse, a crack in the facade of a man torn between the person he wants to be and the one he's become. There are even tears in his eyes. I really can't believe this – from me worrying that he could go for me or perhaps break something, instead, he's practically crying. 'I do love you, you know.'

'Well, you've got a funny way of showing it. Look how you were with us all on Friday morning — shouting and swearing and carrying on. All because you hadn't been paid. Like it was *our* fault.'

'I was hungover, I know it's no excuse, but...' His voice trails off as he slaps his hand heavily beside the crystal glass in front of him. 'Please don't leave me.' He raises his eyes to meet mine. 'Please?'

'Have you eaten?' If I can get some food down him, it will sink him for a while. It always does after he's been drinking. I know the drill – beer, food, sleep. By cooking him something, I can buy myself at least a couple of hours of peace to straighten my thinking out. Part of me hates it when he's nice to me – at least when he's awful, it's easier to keep my leaving plan at the forefront of my mind and act accordingly.

He shakes his head. 'Not since yesterday.'

'That's just ridiculous. You're a grown man, Justin. When are you going to sort yourself out?'

Annie's already told me that his former wife's name for him was apparently *man-child*. I thought it was awful when she first told me, but now I completely understand.

It's Justin's turn to shrug. 'I'm sorry. But I *am* going to change, you know. And as for this stuff...' He takes another large swig of whiskey and then slams the glass onto the table, the sound echoing in the charged silence. 'I'm going to kick it once and for all. This,' he points at his glass as though it's suddenly diseased, 'combined with my bloody ex-wife, has been my absolute downfall.'

It's the same old story. *Blame the alcohol – blame the ex-wife.* When we first met, I believed *everything* he told me about Lynette – I had no reason not to. How she had an affair and then left him with nothing. She wanted to be the one to leave, he said, so he had no idea about exactly where she'd gone.

She left him in a pile of debt and without a stick of furniture. I can clearly remember the expression in his eyes as he recounted the two years he spent before meeting me. He said it had been a long and tough road to claw his way back to normality from where he was, but that in meeting me, he'd finally got himself there.

'What do you say then?' He reaches across the table for my hand. 'Will you just think about it, Melissa? Please just say you'll give our marriage another go – I promise you won't regret it.'

12

I STARE BACK AT HIM.

'We're married and having a baby together, aren't we?' He continues. 'That's all got to count for *something*, surely?'

The silence hangs between us again. I really don't know what to say to him.

'I can't lose you,' he goes on. 'Without you, I'm *nothing*.'

The bottom line here is that my plan B has gone completely belly up. For now, anyway. And with this stupid virus circling wherever it's circling, we could be stuck in here at least for the next few days. For the baby's sake, I should be staying inside the house – I know I should. I could even be stuck in here for longer than a few days. When we were talking earlier, Annie said the powers that be will probably tell us to stay at home for at least a couple of weeks, just to make sure the current cases remain contained.

I don't like the feeling of Justin's hand over mine and long to tug my hand back. It doesn't feel right any more. He might conveniently forget all the names he's called me when it gets to the morning after but I *never* do. It's no wonder I've become so ground down over the last few months.

If I'm to be honest with myself, I'm beat. Without this virus, I could have stayed somewhere else until I got the keys to the house. But because of my pregnancy and asthma, I'm going *nowhere* by the looks of it.

Staying in these four walls with my drunken and abusive husband is actually preferable to a potentially killer virus that's circulating outside. *What has everything come to?*

I'll just have to do my best to keep Justin sweet for the next few days – and with the children at Rick's, this should be easier. At least that's one saving grace.

'Did you mean what you said before – when you promised you'd stop drinking?' Being here a bit longer would be far more tolerable if he could kick the drink. Or at the very least, cut it right back.

'I'll just have one more while you make me something to eat, then I'll go for a kip for an hour.' He runs his fingers through his receding floppy fringe. 'After that, I'll be a new man.' He grins as I get to my feet.

He's slurring his words. I'd better get something cooking sharpish before one extra drink becomes two. The more he gets down him, the likelier he is to turn on me. For now, he's being alright and I need to keep things this way.

He's gone to bed – thank goodness. He's in a weird sort of mood where he becomes clingier and clingier. He's been begging me not to leave him and saying he can't live without me over and over again. I'm utterly wrung out with it all.

What a bloody day and it's not even over yet. I check my watch. Boris Johnson's announcement is less than an hour away and what he's going to say is anyone's guess.

I sink into the sofa, taking in the photo of Aisla and Ewan above the fireplace from last September. I need to speak to them - that'll help me to feel better. I fish around in my bag for my phone.

It's important to remember to keep it in there, out of sight, and the bag on my person at all times so Justin can't get hold of it. When we got these phones, he set facial recognition on both of them, so we can get into each others.

At the time he said it would be a good thing – if one of us were to ever leave our phone behind, the other would be able to access anything that might be needed. I can't deny that alarm bells were ringing at the time, and now I know why. It's just another way he can check up on me. Not that I've ever had anything to hide before.

I hit the button next to Rick's name and settle back against the cushions. It's nearly dark outside, mirroring how I feel inside. Perhaps I'll feel better when the clocks go forward at the weekend, well I will if the kids are back where they belong. With me.

Rick doesn't answer. I try him again. Still nothing. Great.

> I'd like to speak to the kids before they go to bed if that's OK.

The buttons appear straight away which means he's replying. The pillock. This means he hasn't answered my calls on purpose. He'll know how much I'm suffering, being forcibly parted from Aisla and Ewan like this, yet he doesn't give a toss.

> Can we leave it for tonight Melissa? They're both very unsettled.

> All the more reason I should speak to them then.

> We don't think it's a good idea. Maybe tomorrow.

> WE don't think it's a good idea???? Who is SHE to decide whether I get to speak to MY kids or not!!!

I watch the screen for several minutes. He doesn't reply. I jump up from my seat and storm to the window, yanking the curtains across it. I'm going to have to get something sorted out to get them back. *Tomorrow.* I'll see a solicitor if I have to. They can't bloody do this to me.

I suddenly feel sick. I've got to calm down. I tried to eat a bit of the stir fry I cooked for Justin before but I could barely get anything down. I don't think I've ever felt as stressed in my life.

He said he just wants an hour to sleep off the booze but when he's in drink like this, it can easily be three. That's plenty of time for me to keep looking for houses. If I can get something lined up by tomorrow, I can collect Aisla and Ewan. I guess if all else fails, at least I know there's the one I've already paid the application fee on – even if I have to wait for it. The agent's given me his word that I can have it. If only those bloody people had moved out when they were supposed to.

My phone beeps again.

> It's only me, hon. Just wondering how you're getting on. Did you manage to get the keys? xx

> I wish. Nope – the previous tenant's plans have fallen through so it could be a few more days. xx

> Oh no! What are you going to do? xx

> What choice have I got? I'll have to hang in here until I can get them. xx

Really, I want to tell her that Rick's taken the kids too. But she'd probably *insist* on me staying at the pub then. And much as she means well, I really would feel more vulnerable with her being a nurse and being in daily proximity to the virus, so I don't want to. Besides, I'm sure I can hold things together here, especially if it only ends up being for a few days. As well as that, I wouldn't want to be around Simon. I know for a fact that I'd end up challenging him about what he's done.

> Oh love - are you OK? xx

Yeah. I'm fine. He's had a few to drink so he's in bed sleeping it off. I'm just chilling with a cup of tea. xx

> Did he say anything about what he and Simon were rowing about??? Simon won't even talk about it! xx

Not really. I got the impression it was about some owed money, that's all. xx

I hate lying, but I can hardly tell her that *my* husband appears to be blackmailing *her* husband over an illicit weekend he's recently enjoyed.

We continue with a few more texts about the virus and the impending announcement and I finish up by telling her I'll text her again tomorrow.

'Is it on yet?' Justin appears in the doorway, with his hair on end. There's a wet dab on his boxers and sleep lines all over his face. Gone are the pristine white Calvin Klein's he used to wear before we were married. I fancied this man so much until three months ago. Now I've barely any idea what I could have possibly seen in him.

'Two minutes,' I reply, averting my gaze from his crotch and hoping the look of disgust on my face isn't too obvious. 'I didn't think you'd be awake yet.'

'I said I only wanted an hour, didn't I?' He throws himself onto the sofa next to me. 'I bet you'd have left me up there all night if you'd had *your* way.'

'It's starting.' We both stiffen as we turn to the screen.

The prime minister talks about the virus and what needs to be done, what the government's going to do, and the impact on the NHS if it gets any worse.

But it's the words *you must stay at home* that cause me to do a double take. As the flickering images of the prime minister fill the room, the ticking clock on the wall seems to echo the urgency of the unfolding crisis.

My chest tightens. 'He can't mean stay at home *completely,*' I say. 'We'll all be like prisoners. I'm not doing it.'

'Shhh.' Justin raises his hand like he always does when he wants to listen to something.

I listen peripherally as the prime minister lays out what we can do, and most importantly what we *can't.*

'He's closing *everything,* more or less.' I clasp my hand to my mouth. 'Shops, gyms, pubs, oh my God. And have you heard that? We're allowed out on our own for a walk for ONE hour a day!'

'Melissa, please, I'm trying to listen.' Justin sits forward on the sofa.

It quickly becomes clear that this extremely weird set of instructions is even to be enshrined in law. We can be *legally* prevented from meeting our friends. Even if I wanted to go and stay with Annie or someone from work, I'm no longer allowed to. I can't believe what's going on here, it's like we've suddenly found ourselves in the middle of a strange dystopian film.

'We will beat the coronavirus and we will beat it together,' Johnson finally concludes.

'So there we have it.' Justin leans into the cushions, looking almost pleased about what's going on. 'You couldn't leave me even if you wanted to.'

13

SINCE I'VE BEEN pregnant I've been getting up earlier and earlier –
usually even before the kids are awake.

The kids.

Remembering where they are, but most importantly, *why* they
are there, almost winds me for a moment. And now, with all these
new rules, it sounds like I'd struggle to have them back with me
anyway. There's nothing else for it – I'm simply going to have to be
warrior-strong and get myself through this time without them. And
I'm going to have to make doubly sure I'm able to get out of this
house as soon as it's possible.

In the meantime, I'm going to have to try and act normal in
front of Justin, as though I *am* giving him another chance – if only
for the sake of keeping the peace.

I settle onto the sofa with a cup of tea. I can tell from the pinky-
peach sunrise and clear sky that it's going to be another scorcher of
a day.

It's as if the sunshine is Mother Nature's way of compensating
us for the loss of normality and freedom we're going to be forced to

endure for the next three weeks. *Three weeks!* Aisla and Ewan will have forgotten what I look like during that time.

I'm gutted about the situation but somehow, I'm going to have to try and put it to the back of my mind or it will drive me insane. I know they'll be well looked after while they're with their dad and stepmum and that we can make up for lost time when these three weeks of 'staying at home' are over and done with.

The house is swathed in silence – I only hope it stays this way for at least a couple more hours. It's going to be necessary to find some things to keep me occupied – I might look for some pregnancy yoga on YouTube for my mornings until I can go back to work. And there's bound to be other stuff I can learn about or make. That's if Justin will give me the peace and space to get on with my own thing. If only I'd got into that house yesterday, I could have been using this enforced time away from work to get it sorted and make it lovely for me and the kids.

I check my watch. They should be up by now so I'm going to call them.

Just as I think it's going to go to voicemail, Rick answers. 'Don't you think it's a bit early Melissa?' His voice is thick with sleep and it's hard not to imagine him lying beside my nemesis, Cara.

'I only want to say a quick hello to the kids. Come on Rick, I haven't seen them since Friday.' I can hear them larking about somewhere in the background so he can't pretend that they're still sleeping.

He grunts but sounds as though he's getting out of bed. I hear Cara's muffled voice but can't make out what she's saying. It's probably just as well.

'It's your mum,' Rick says after a few moments.

'Mum!' Aisla shrieks into the phone. 'Have you heard what's happening? We can't go back to school and we've got to stay in the house and we can't even see our friends!'

'I know, sweetheart. It's all very strange, isn't it?'

'I'm scared I'll catch the virus too. I couldn't even get to sleep last night for worrying about it.'

'You'll be fine, as long as you follow all the rules for a couple of weeks.'

'But when will we see you?' She suddenly sounds crestfallen as if the realisation we're going to be apart has only just hit her.

'As soon as we can, I promise. In the meantime, you just need to be good for your dad and try not to fall out with Ewan too much.' I force a laugh, even though it's breaking my heart just to hear her voice. But she's fine. They're both better off where they are than with me for the time being. 'Is Ewan there, love?'

'Yes, he's here. He's waiting to speak to you.'

'Just give me the phone. I want to talk to Mum.' Ewan sounds just like his father – impatient.

'Hi, Mum.'

'It's so good to hear your voice. How are you doing?'

'We're OK. But we're missing you.'

Tears prickle at the back of my eyes. 'Me too.' I must keep it together. If Ewan gets the slightest whiff that I'm struggling, he'll keep worrying about me. 'But I'm OK sweetheart. We're going to have to be separated for now but we'll see each other as soon as we can.'

'But Mum, that could be *ages*.'

'We've got to follow the rules love, and because I've got the baby and my asthma, I've got to follow the rules even more.'

'But what about—?'

I know what he's going to say so I jump in first. 'Everything's OK here, Ewan. I've got lots to keep me busy. What about you? How are you and Aisla going to amuse yourselves?'

I don't want him to have to think about Justin and this is not the time for me to broach the fact that they got upset at school about it all. I'll talk to them properly when I get them back.

He launches into a list of all the things they've got planned, baking, board games, building a tree house and watching films. I might not think a great deal of Cara but I can tell they're in good hands. After chatting for a few minutes, we say our goodbyes and hang up.

After they've gone, I'm left with an overwhelming sense of loneliness, a heavy weight settling in the silence. To dispel the solitude, I flick the TV on, craving any distraction from the echoing emptiness.

14

'Who were *you* talking to before?'

I twist in my seat at the sound of Justin's voice, my heart suddenly racing at a hundred miles an hour.

'Just the kids. Why?'

'Is this how it's going to be for the next three weeks?' Still in his baggy boxers, he strides into the lounge and flings himself onto the sofa where I've been absently staring at the TV. 'You, on the phone to them every five minutes?'

'Why, what's the problem?'

'We should be focusing on *us*, that's what. I'd hoped we could spend some proper time together.' He still hasn't shaved and looks even worse than he did last night. 'We're supposed to be making a go of things, aren't we?'

'We'll be spending *lots* of time together.' I try to keep the edge of despair from my voice. In all honesty, I still can't believe this being forced to remain in our homes is even happening.

'I've just been listening to the news again. They're talking about this new furlough scheme.'

'This new *what* scheme?' At least he's instigating a normal conversation. He can be at his absolute worst in the morning. Often because all his regrets from the previous day spill into his hangover.

'Furlough. The government will pay eighty per cent of your wages. That's if it all goes through like they're on about. So hopefully this means we'll be alright for money after all.'

I get a whiff of his pungent breath as he speaks. My sense of smell seems to have been heightened since I've become pregnant which, in this instance, is not a good thing.

'So you'll need to set that up to be paid into the joint account so I can access it too.'

'If it's through *my* work, it'll go into *my* bank account.'

'So what am I supposed to do?' His jaw tightens. 'Rot? I'm only asking you to move things into the joint account so we can share what we've got.'

My eyes fill with tears as I look away and fix my gaze back on the TV screen.

'So you'll set it up then?'

I sniff. 'I'll have to wait to hear something from work first.'

My mind races as we sit in silence for a few moments. I'm well and truly trapped here. Whatever money I manage to claim or get hold of, Justin's going to take control of by the sounds of it. I don't know what to do.

'You're quiet, aren't you?'

'I'm just watching this. Just look.' I point at the screen, no longer able to hold onto my tears as I realise what's happening. An elderly woman and a woman my age are waving to each other through a window. 'This is what I'm going to be reduced to when I want to see *my* mum.'

'You're going nowhere near that care home.'

'Why?'

'I'm not having you pick up the virus. That's my baby you're carrying too.'

'But it's not as if I'll be allowed anywhere near her. I'll just be outside.'

'I said no, Melissa.'

'But she'll think I've abandoned her.'

'You turn up outside her window and it'll probably confuse her even more. Just leave it, will you? She's being looked after, isn't she?' He leans forward for the cup of tea I've made myself. 'Don't mind if I do. My mouth feels as though something's died in it this morning.'

Just as I'm about to protest further, I have a sense of being watched. I shield my eyes against the brilliance of the sun-drenched window, inadvertently catching a glimpse of our new neighbour, her curious gaze fixed on our window. She must notice me, for she instantly turns to look the other way.

Not that there's much to see out on the square this morning. Outside, the gate to the playground stands padlocked, a stark reminder of these unprecedented times. The once lively square now wears a deserted look, its usual vibrancy muted by the absence of children playing. Everyone must be saving their hour of permitted outdoor exercise until later in the day.

'What are you looking at.' Justin follows my gaze. The woman is at a perfect vantage point and seems able to see straight into our house.

'I'm not having that.' Justin jumps up from the sofa so abruptly that he slops my tea all over the table.

'You're not having *what*? What are you doing?'

He lurches towards the window. 'What does it look like I'm doing? Nosy cow!' He yanks the curtains together and then turns to rejoin me on the sofa. But as the letterbox rattles, he stops in his tracks and we look at each other.

'Do you think it's even safe to touch things that are posted through?' I ask. 'Just think of all the other gates and letterboxes the postman will have been to. The virus can live on things, can't it?'

'I'll wash my hands straight after,' he replies as he heads from the lounge into the hallway.

I rack my brains to think if there's a possibility of anything arriving today that I wouldn't want him to see. I've put in applications for several credit cards and personal loans which have all been turned down flat. No doubt they'll all be writing me a *thanks but no thanks* sort of letter at some point. However, he returns clutching something which just looks like a flyer.

'What is it?' I try to peer over his shoulder as he sits back down.

'That do-gooder from a couple of doors down has set up some sort of stupid Facebook group.'

'You mean Diane?' I catch the words *Village Greeners Helping Each Other* before he screws it up and tosses it into the fireplace. 'What have you done that for?' I say. 'I think it's a nice idea to have a group for the square.'

I'll fish it back out later when he's out of the way and have a proper look. 'I thought you were going to wash your hands.'

I sigh as he leaves the room. The next twenty days until we have the possibility of these restrictions being lifted are stretching out before me like a tightrope. I feel as if I'm walking on one as well.

The breakfast programme we've got on has now switched to a discussion about homeschooling kids. If I'd had Aisla and Ewan here to help with some schoolwork, it would have kept me busy and given me a sense of purpose. Instead, bloody Cara will be doing the honours. It's hard not to feel resentful at times – I've often hated her for stealing my life and right now – it feels as though she has, more than ever.

'Everyone's stuck in their homes until the next announcement, no matter what.' He returns to the room, shaking water from his hands. 'What good is a poxy *Facebook group* going to do?' He frowns as he points the remote at the TV. 'We'll have this thing off, shall we? I think we've heard enough about the Coronavirus for the time being.'

'There'll be those who are *really* vulnerable living on the square. They might need some shopping organising, or their medicine picking up.' I'm suddenly relieved that at least my mum's being looked after and that she's safe. The care home stopped visitors going in a couple of weeks ago, and I've found out from their newsletter that they've got staff living in there for the time being, to limit contact with the outside world.

If Mum was still alone at home I'd be in a constant state of worry. 'There'll be people *totally* on their own, you know. It's a time for us all to come together if you ask me.'

'We don't need to be getting involved with any of that.' Justin crosses one muscular leg over the other and I wonder if he's even planning to get dressed today. But despite what he drinks, Justin manages to stay in good shape. Probably from being up and down ladders as a decorator – when he goes to work, that is. 'You should know what I'm like by now – I prefer us to keep ourselves completely to ourselves – it's far easier that way.'

'It'll help me to get to know some more of the neighbours if we join in with the group,' I protest. 'I've been living here for over a year and I still only know a couple of them.'

'What do you want to get to know the neighbours for?'

'It could be fun, this Facebook group. There's always Facetime to have a proper conversation with people.'

'Am I not enough for you?' He looks hurt. 'This could be a great opportunity for the two of us.' He points from himself to me. 'While the kids are with their dad and before the baby comes along, we could use this time to fix our marriage.'

He looks so earnest, it's almost laughable. He thinks he's got me where he wants me. Perhaps he has me trapped here in body. But certainly not in heart or mind.

'What do you say? We can start again and get back to how things were like before.'

'I guess we can try.' It's got to be the least enthusiastic sentence I've ever uttered.

'I'd say we can do a lot more than *try*.' He slams the palm of his hand against the arm of the sofa, making me jump.

One thing's for certain – I can't bear to just sit here with him all day. These four walls are beginning to close in on me already. If I can just get out of here for short periods, I can start to formulate a plan of how I'm going to survive until this 'stay at home' order is lifted. And what I'm going to do beyond that.

'I'm off to get changed, then I'm going for a walk,' I tell him as I rise from the sofa.

'You can't.' Justin's voice is firm and demanding. He catches the back of my dressing gown as I walk past him. '*You're* one of the people who's supposed to be shielding.'

'You heard the speech last night.' I shake myself free of his grasp. 'An hour is allowed for exercise. I can even go to the supermarket if I want to.'

'I'll be sorting all that.' His expression is firm and resolute. 'The once-a-day rule is for people who *aren't* classed as vulnerable. Which *isn't* you, right?'

I sink to the arm of the chair facing him. 'But I'll stay away from other people,' I tell him. I feel like Ewan arguing for an extra ten minutes of playing out time. 'I can't just stay cooped up in here twenty-four-seven.'

'You've heard how easily the virus spreads,' he replies. 'What happens if you touch a gate handle or pick up the same packet in a shop as someone who's got it? You've no idea *who* has touched *what* before you.'

'But where's the line drawn?' I reply. 'No matter what, we've still got to receive post and shopping into the house.'

'We'll disinfect it all,' he replies. 'And I'll take care of the post. I've told you I'm going to change Melissa – just let me look after you.'

I flop into the armchair. There seems little point whatsoever in getting dressed. I'm stuck in here for the foreseeable. This house is now my prison and my husband has become my jailer.

15

'YOU SHOULD BE PUTTING your feet up.' Justin raises his gaze from his laptop. 'Honestly Melissa – treat this time as a chance to take a break.'

I pause from scrubbing at the cooker to study him. His fingers drum a light rhythm on the table, and a subtle smile tugs at the corners of his mouth. He's in a better mood than he's been in for weeks.

'I find cleaning relaxing,' I reply. 'I might as well be doing something useful.'

I don't know why I'm scrubbing at an oven that I'm planning on leaving behind in the not-too-distant future, but I'll do anything to keep busy and to pass the time.

'I might go through all the drawers when I've done this,' I say. 'Some of them are so jam-packed that it's impossible to open them.'

Plus, it's a good opportunity to make sure I've got everything that's mine or the kids out of them.

'Well leave my drawer alone.' He nods towards it, a hint of tension in his voice. 'I'll go through it *myself* sometime.'

'I don't mind – I'm happy to do it.'

'No, *really*. I need to go through it myself – there's all sorts in there. Anyway, get those things off.' He points at my rubber gloves. 'You've been at it all morning. Come on - I'll make you a cuppa, shall I?'

He's certainly wearing clothes more appropriate for the sunshine today, he's in shorts and a t-shirt, whereas I'm still in my yoga clothes. Everything just feels meaningless at the moment, including choosing what to wear.

He rises from his chair and makes his way across the kitchen. 'Come on Melissa.' He reaches for one of my gloves but I tug my hand away. 'It's OK, I can manage.'

I'm shocked when he leans forward and plants a kiss on my forehead. It momentarily reminds me of a time when things were happier between us. I resist the urge to wipe the kiss away even though it feels like it's burning into my skin.

'I'll do whatever it takes to get us back on track, you know.' He doesn't take his eyes off me. 'I think we should do lots of talking over the next few days, don't you?'

I tug at my other glove and turn away from him. 'I once suggested counselling Justin, but you didn't want to go.'

'We don't need counselling.' His voice changes and I worry for a moment that I've said the wrong thing.

If he *had* agreed to counselling, perhaps we might have stood a chance. And I'll always wonder if we'd have fared better if he'd given himself the chance to properly get over his divorce from Lynette, before pressuring me to take things so fast with him.

He places a mug of tea on the table in front of me, sliding a plate of chocolate biscuits beside it. After not sleeping well for nights on end, I suddenly feel exhausted, not to mention, in rather a daze from him suddenly being kind and attentive.

'Thank you.' I cross one leg over the other, glancing down to notice I've ruined my yoga pants, the splatters of oven cleaner contrasting against the fabric. I suppose I'd better get changed. I felt chilly and miserable when I first got up this morning but perhaps I'll feel better if I shower and change into something cooler.

'Get those down you as well.' He nudges the plate towards me. 'You're eating for two, remember? You seem to be losing weight when surely, you should be gaining it by now?'

I don't feel remotely hungry but I should acknowledge his effort, otherwise he might get irritated. So I lean forward and take one. 'It's just because of the sickness.' This isn't the time to tell him how stress always kills my appetite – and it's something he's wholly responsible for.

He lowers himself to the armchair facing me, with what looks like concern swimming in his eyes. They've been steely and grey lately, but an unexpected warmth infiltrates them now. It's something so alien that it brings tears to my own eyes. I've really got to be careful here – my hormones are all over the place and my emotional state is flitting up and down like a yo-yo. Yes, it makes a change that he's being nice to me today, but nothing will ever detract from the cracks in our relationship, a web of fractures as intricate as shattered glass, leading me to the inevitable decision I've been forced to make.

'I do love you, Melissa.' He tilts my chin in his fingers which forces me to look directly at him whether I want to or not. And I don't want to. 'I've been an absolute pig to you.' His voice wobbles.

'We don't need to go down—'

'Yes, we do. Just let me say this.'

I suck on a piece of biscuit, turning the sugary taste around in my mouth as I fight the urge to cry. Now I've let myself sit down, I feel absolutely wrung out and I can't cope with Justin. Whether he's being abusive, kind, or indifferent, I just wish he'd leave me alone.

'I'm going to make everything up to you, I promise. You deserve so much better than I've been treating you.'

'I don't know what went wrong.' *My* voice wobbles now. What I need now more than anything is a hug. But not from him. My mother's face enters my head. I have to see her – I *need* to see her.

'It's all me – it's been totally me,' he replies. He leans forward as if trying to get closer to me. 'I guess that I've been spooked by how much I love you. After losing Cameron like I did, I've become scared of losing you as well.'

'I don't understand.' I peer at him from beneath my fringe while hoping he doesn't try to get any closer. 'Surely you must realise that your behaviour could only *ever* push me away.'

'I know.' He hangs his head. 'And I know I've been drinking like a fish since Christmas. It was all after what Cameron said to me. I can't handle him not wanting to know me.' His voice cracks and he looks towards the bay window.

The crystal vase we were given on our wedding day from Annie and Simon catches the late morning sunlight, casting delicate prisms across the room. The window frames a view of the empty square outside, a stark reminder of our isolated situation.

'But it's been this way between you and Cameron for as long as I've known you.'

'I've been burying my head in the sand about it, haven't I?' He stares at the carpet. 'I only let it all get to me after that telephone call. I've taken it out on the last person I should be hurting.' He looks at me again, his eyes more sorrowful than I've ever seen them.

'Do you think you can forgive me?'

16

I STARE BACK AT HIM. 'Let's just see how things go, shall we?' It's about the best I can give him. 'It's been a rough ride.'

'I know I'm asking you to forgive what I can barely even forgive myself for.' He clasps his hands together as though praying for something. 'And I've ruined what should have been the happiest months of our lives.'

Suddenly, he drops from where he's sitting on the chair onto the floor. *What the hell is he doing?* I watch as he shuffles across the carpet, before arriving at my feet. He reaches up and rests his hand against my belly. A gesture that should feel warm and comforting is an unwelcome intrusion, sending shivers of discomfort down my spine. It's all I can do not to slap his hand away from me.

'Our baby,' he says after a few endless moments. 'I'm going to make her so proud to have me as her daddy. And you'll be even prouder to have me as your husband.'

I don't think so.

'What if it's a boy?' He's done this ever since my positive test. He's always been adamant I'm carrying a girl. It bothered me in the beginning, but now I don't care what he does or doesn't think.

'I doubt it will be. I can't lie though...' Thankfully, he moves his hand and looks down at the carpet. 'Having a girl would be *far* easier for me. Less of a reminder of Cameron. A daughter would *never* reject me like he has.'

Talking about Cameron probably isn't a good way to go. Not if it puts him back into one of the dark moods I'm so keen to alleviate. Therefore, it's time to change the subject. Plus, his proximity is still far too close for my liking. I slither away from him, a silent retreat from the encroaching darkness that his presence brings. 'Well, if you don't want me scrubbing the oven,' I turn a circle on the carpet. 'I'd better find something else to be getting on with.'

'We could make a start on the baby's room?' The level of enthusiasm in his voice surprises me. 'I've plenty of gloss and emulsion in the shed,' he continues, 'and I helped myself to a colour injection before I was sacked the other day. You *did* want yellow, didn't you?'

I nod. I guess it can't hurt for him to be getting on with that. It'll keep him out of *my* hair. Being busy will hopefully keep him away from the drink as well – not that he's got a great deal of the stuff left.

He has, so far, honoured my requests not to venture to the supermarket to stock up. It's far too risky and I think I've persuaded him that we can hang on until public demand for delivery slots dies down. We've still got a fridge and freezer full of food so it's not as though we're going to starve. And because the kids aren't here, what we've got will last even longer.

'*You* can get started if you want,' I say. 'But have you seen it out there? Just look at that lovely blue sky.' I point at the window. 'I want to make the most of it. I might sort the shed out.'

Again, I can make sure I've got the children's stuff in there piled to one side and ready to easily transport out of here. If I'd left on Monday, when I was supposed to, I was so disorganised that I think I'd have left lots of our things behind.

Justin follows my gaze to the window. 'I'd rather you didn't actually.'

The woman from the flat is chatting to Monica, one of the

neighbours. They're both standing at their gates. The rule is to keep two metres apart, at all times. But even two metres would feel too close for me at the moment.

'I'd prefer you to sit down and put your feet up,' he says.

'Oh, OK then.' The last thing I want is to do or say *anything* that might trigger any sign of a negative mood in him. Not when he seems to have got up this morning having had a personality transplant. Hopefully, it will continue, but even if it doesn't, I need to make the most of the respite for as long as it lasts.

'Good, that's settled. It'll do you good to relax for a change. Especially while you haven't got the kids to run around after.'

As if I need reminding. 'I just hope I don't get bored.' I perch on the edge of the window sill.

'I've been thinking about that,' he replies. 'And I've had a few ideas for things to do while we have to stay inside.'

'Such as?'

'Well, there's the obvious, of course.' He winks at me. It's a gesture that used to make me melt once upon a time. But that feels like a lifetime ago. 'When you're feeling up to it again, of course,' he adds quickly. This is a turn-up for the books. It normally infuriates him when he perceives any sort of rejection from me in the bedroom department. Let's see how long it lasts.

'I was thinking we could learn a language together – maybe Spanish,' he says. 'Then we'll be all ready for the holiday I'm going to take you on as soon as we're able to go.'

Yeah right. I won't ask how he's planning to pay for it.

'And what about learning to dance? Properly, I mean. Do you remember what I said at our wedding, how I wished we'd learned some proper steps instead of just spinning in circles at the centre of the dance floor?'

'Yeah, I remember.' I glance at our wedding photograph next to the vase. Something else that feels like a lifetime ago.

'So now's our chance. There must be a ton of videos around to teach beginners like us.'

'We'll see.'

'I could teach you how to play chess too. Another thing we could do together.'

'Yeah, maybe. Or I could have a go at painting – see if it's me Aisla gets her artistic talent from.'

At the mention of her name, my face must fall. His certainly does.

'Is being alone with me for three weeks really so bad?'

I shake my head. I don't trust myself to speak.

'Tell me the truth, Melissa. Are the kids staying with Rick because of the *virus* or because of *me*?'

Bloody hell. He's more astute than I gave him credit for. 'The virus,' I reply, hoping my face won't give me away. I've always been a rubbish liar. 'To protect *me*.' I lower my gaze.

'OK – Let's just go forward now, shall we?' He sits beside me on the window sill, and the subtle fragrance of shaving cream and soap replaces the usual acrid odour of alcohol.

'When all this is over,' he declares, 'we're going to get Aisla and Ewan back home, the baby will be born and then we're going to be a proper happy family.'

The irony of his words lingers in the air. But, in this moment I almost believe him.

17

ONE WEEK LATER

THE SHRILL BIRDSONG pierces through my drowsiness, a relentless reminder that morning has come too soon. I long for the comfort of darkness, for the respite it provides from the endless days stretching ahead.

At least I've woken in Aisla's room rather than beside *him*. To avoid extra grief at bedtime, I pretended I was feeling sickly and didn't want to disturb him by being up and down through the night.

The truth was that I couldn't bear sleeping beside the stench of stale whiskey. I couldn't bear sleeping beside him full stop. He polished off the last half of his final bottle last night and was soon ranting once again about the various wrongdoings of his ex-wife. His sobriety and false promises have lasted barely a week. He got as far as stripping wallpaper from two walls of the so-called nursery and that was it.

When I challenged him about giving in to the drink again, he blamed Lynette. Then he went onto Cameron. And lastly, of course, he went on to blame me.

I can hardly bear to face another day of this monotony. It's day number eleven. Each day feels like the one before and there's little comfort in knowing that tomorrow will be exactly like today.

Aisla's room, adorned with fairy lights and posters of her favourite pop stars, feels both nostalgic and melancholic. Most of her belongings are packed in boxes in the loft as they await an uncertain future.

I'd give *anything* right now to see Aisla wearing her fluffy purple dressing gown, which hangs forlornly from the hook on the back of the door.

I close my eyes again, imagining her hair, wet and strawberry-scented from a bath while she leans into me for a snuggle. The heat of tears prods at the back of my eyes. I miss them both so much.

The stuffed animals on the shelf stare back at me, their plastic eyes holding memories I wish I could forget. When I helped Justin paint this room, I thought we were here to stay. He'd told me I looked 'cute' while splattered in paint so I dabbed some on his forehead. In the end, there was more paint on us than on the walls and the kids were laughing their heads off.

It's no good. I'm going to have to get moving. I can't let the situation grind me down any more than it already has done. I just need to keep myself strong and ready for all that I have to do when the restrictions are lifted.

Since we locked down, Justin's veered between being overbearingly 'loving' towards me and trying to control what I do and who I talk to. Now he's fallen off the wagon, who knows what's in store for me?

But at least he hasn't been abusive or violent. I pray this isn't to come – especially not when there's nowhere for me to run.

~

I tiptoe down the stairs and fill a glass, taking care to allow the water not to run fast enough to make any noise.

The birdsong appears to have grown louder over the last few days – though maybe it's the absence of traffic that's enabling me to truly hear it. I'm going to have to get out for a walk today – no matter how 'vulnerable' I'm supposed to be. I won't touch a thing out there – in fact, I'll even wear gloves and a scarf over my nose. And I won't go anywhere near another soul.

But I've *got* to get out. If I set off before Justin gets up, he can't do anything to stop me. I can give Mum and the kids another call while I'm walking and speak to them without Justin hanging around, listening in.

But first, while he's still asleep, I'll do some yoga – another thing Justin doesn't seem to like me doing. Anything that takes me into my own space and away from him, he doesn't approve of.

I pull on some joggers and a t-shirt from the ironing pile and twist my hair into a bun at the top of my head.

The sunshine spills in like liquid gold as I open the curtains. Justin has insisted on keeping them closed. He reckons it's to prevent 'the nosy neighbours,' as he calls them, from looking in. I miss Diane giving me a wave as she passes. But I don't miss the watchful eyes of the new neighbour. As I recall Justin's debt to her, I think *she's* the main reason for his irritation. After all, I know for a fact that he's barely got any money at the moment.

It also feels good to roll my yoga mat across the carpet. It's been a week since I've been anywhere near it after Justin last complained.

I find what's been described as a *soothing* pregnancy yoga session to do on YouTube. As I lay down on my mat, the soft instrumental music and the instructor's calming voice fills my ears.

If Justin stays in bed until at least the same time as he did yesterday, the day might be more bearable. The instructor invites me to stretch my limbs like a starfish and as I do, for the first time, I feel the baby move.

It's just a flutter but definitely there. For a moment, I almost forget about the situation and have the urge to rush upstairs to tell Justin – to invite him to place a hand on my belly and feel it for himself. I could with Rick when I was having Aisla and Ewan. But I can't this time. Something inside me sags as I remember that I'm in this on my own.

As I move from warrior one to warrior two, I allow my gaze to roam across the square. It's usually bustling with the energy of communal life, but apart from a solitary woman throwing a ball for her dog, it's completely deserted. At least, I should be safe when I venture outside.

The sense of being watched is back again. I avert my eyes to the neighbour's second-floor window and for a moment, on some level, sense a connection with her. She seems to be on her own up there and I guess, that like me, she's probably got nothing better to do than to people-watch, even when the most exciting thing they're doing is attempting morning yoga.

I drop my arms back to my sides and lean towards the window. I should acknowledge her so I wave. But instead of waving back, she drops the curtain down and disappears. Perhaps she's embarrassed, having been caught staring into my window.

18

After yoga, I take my tea and toast into the garden and lower myself to my favourite spot on the wall. Today marks eleven days since I've left the house. As I chew on my toast, I open the news app on my phone while I can look at it in peace. Justin, when he's not too busy pouring whatever he can lay his hands on down his neck, constantly berates me for being glued to the news.

I'm watching for a sign, *any sign*, that this situation won't go on beyond next Monday when another announcement is due to be made.

According to the headlines, the virus could be already 'peaking' in Spain. As I move to the next headline, I gasp. The latest death figures have been released *here*. More than three thousand people have died from the virus in one day. Which is double what it was four days ago. I can't lie – I'm terrified. Perhaps I won't go for that walk after all. It's spreading like the bubonic plague.

I hope and pray Rick's shielding the kids from any risk of catching it. Usually, he just passes the phone to them as soon as I call, so I'll have to ask for a word with him next time. Hopefully, Rick and Cara are adhering to the rules as much as I am. I've accepted that the children are not going to be returned to me just yet, and no matter how much this hurts, I know it's for the best with the way things are.

I just wish I'd given in to Ewan's pleas for a mobile phone at Christmas, instead of telling him he'd have to wait for his birthday. I've always said he could only have one when he gets to high school age but if I'd given in, at least I'd be able to keep in constant contact with him instead of having to rely on Rick *allowing* them to speak to me.

I scroll down to another news report. They're making plans for football stadiums and closed-down hotels to be used as makeshift hospitals and morgues. *Oh my God!* I wonder how Annie's coping. The numbers have increased so fast, that there's bound to be even more cases at her hospital by now. While she's on my mind – I'll drop her a text.

> It's only me. Just checking in with you to make sure you're alright. xx

> I've just finished a night shift. It's carnage. ICU is full to bursting. But I'm OK. Anyway, never mind me, how are you coping, being holed up with HIM?? I hope things are bearable. xx

> It's not been too bad. He's been off the drink. Well, until last night anyway. So I'm just keeping out of his way as much as I can. xx

> Did you ever find out what the row was that he had with Simon? xx

Gosh, she's still thinking about *that*. Simon's betrayal is the *last* thing she needs to know about with all she's got going on at work.

No, he never mentioned anything. He probably owes him some money or something. Which reminds me. How well do you know the new tenant in Simon's old flat? Justin owes HER some money for a job he never did.

I don't know her at all. Is there ANYONE Justin doesn't owe money to?!!! Anyway, I'm off to bed. I'll drop you a line over the next couple of days. xx

OK. Take care. xx

'How are you all doing Melissa?' Diane calls across our two dividing fences. 'Are the kids managing to keep themselves occupied?'

'They're with their dad,' I reply, my voice as flat as a pancake. She must know full well after all this time that they aren't here – she's obviously being nosy.

'Oh? Why's that then? Isn't their dad out at work?'

'Hardly anyone's *out at work* at the moment,' I reply. 'How are *you* anyway?' I don't want to talk about Aisla and Ewan not being here. Not to anyone. The situation is crucifying me enough as it is.

'Oh, you know me. I'm just getting on with as much as I can. I was glad to see you've joined the Facebook group.'

I glance up at the bedroom window from which the curtain is flapping in the breeze. I need to keep my voice down. 'I joined at the weekend,' I reply.

I haven't heard any movement from upstairs this morning so hopefully, Justin's still fast asleep. 'But there's not a lot I can do to help anyone while I'm in this predicament.' Resting a hand on my belly, I smile at her.

'It should be others helping *you*.' She points at me. 'You're asthmatic as well, if I'm remembering correctly, aren't you?'

'How do you know that?'

'Don't you remember that time when we got chatting?'

'That could be any number of times.' I say. I do like Diane and it's nice to be conversing with a different human being other than

Justin for once. Once I got over my annoyance at her meddling when I was moving in, I realised it was because she genuinely seemed to care. Plus, there's something quite comforting about Diane. Maybe, with her grey-bobbed hair and brightly-coloured pinny, there's something about her which reminds me of my mother before dementia wormed itself within her.

'It was as we waited for our prescriptions at the chemist that time,' she replies.

'Oh yes - I remember now. Who knows when we'll be *allowed* to stand in the chemist again.' It's weird how something so ordinary is now something so completely forbidden.

'It's a shame the children aren't around at the moment.' She's not letting this go. 'They're all drawing pictures to put in their windows, have you seen them all? To say thank you to the NHS.'

'I haven't been out anywhere.'

'No, of course not. I'm sorry.'

My heart sinks as Justin's angry voice emanates from somewhere within the house.

'Erm, I'm going to have to go.'

It doesn't sound as though he's shouting to me, more that he's arguing with someone on the phone. Whichever it is, it doesn't bode well. I should have known the 'nicer' side of him wouldn't last long.

'Are *you* OK in there?' Diane wears a concerned expression as she leans over her fence and into next door's garden. They'd probably shoo her back onto her own side if they were to come outside now.

Diane nearly *always* looks concerned when she speaks to me. 'Like I've tried telling you before, we *all* know what your husband's like.' She jerks her head in the direction of the upstairs of my house as his shouting continues.

It's the first time that she's gone down this road of conversation since I gave her short shrift last year. Now that I've seen Justin's true colours for myself, I can hardly dismiss her again. Perhaps I need to pick this woman's brains. After all, I've only ever heard Justin's side of the story. 'What do you mean?'

'Just that we all heard what he was like with Lynette. And judging from what I'm still hearing, he hasn't learned his lesson.'

'Annie at the pub's told me bits and pieces.'

'She didn't know Lynette though. Not like we did.' Diane gives me a knowing look. 'I don't think she ever even met her.'

I sigh. 'I'd better find out what's going on in there.'

'If you need any help.' Diane leans so far into next door's garden that she looks like she could topple over the fence. 'You know where to come, don't you? Anytime.'

'Thanks. But I'm sure I'll be fine.' As I turn to face the house, I mutter under my breath, 'I think.'

Whether it's his hangover or his telephone conversation that's caused it, Justin's definitely in one of his darker moods again. And if he catches me out here, talking to Diane, I risk adding fuel to his fire.

19

***

'YOU'RE LYING, he yells at whichever poor sod he's arguing with.

I lean against the bannister at the bottom of the stairs, holding my breath. There's a pause before he shouts again. 'I know *full well* you're good for it.'

Then another pause. The whole square must be able to hear him bawling. Then, as though he can read my mind, he slams the bedroom window – the sound reverberates through the house, and sends a shiver through me.

Exhaling a heavy breath, my eyes fixate on the sign next to the front door, its hollow promise mocking my chaos.

In our happy home, hearts are full, and smiles are contagious.

Yeah right.

'I can't wait that long Simon, you know I can't. I need that money this week.'

'Well you should have thought about that before you went behind your missus's back, shouldn't you?'

'Well that's not very nice, is it – you're definitely the first *friend* who's ever wished me dead.'

The tone of his voice darkens. 'Like I've already told you, you've got until the end of the week before she gets to know what you're really made of.'

'Five grand and I'm off your back. That's all it's going to take.' His voice takes on a flippant edge. His tone is so casual, that he could be simply requesting the loan of a tenner.

'Because you'll have my word. I'll send them *all* to you to destroy.'

'I don't give a shit about any of that. You've got until Friday, do you hear me?'

Justin suddenly appears at the top of the stairs. Simon must have ended the call, but clearly, before I realised and could get out of the way.

'Have you been listening in to my *private* telephone conversation?' The tone of his voice says it all.

'I erm, I was coming up to see if you wanted a brew, that's all.'

'Don't bloody lie to me. We both know you're a crap liar.' He tightens the cord of his dressing gown. 'You were eavesdropping on my conversation, weren't you?'

I know that frenzied look in his eyes. It's the look that says *I'm going to be drinking whatever booze I can lay my hands on for my breakfast today.*

I step backwards as he descends the stairs.

'What's up with you? Why are you flinching like that?' He stops on the second step. He's towering over me even more than he usually would.

'I was just moving out of your way, that's all.'

'You really can't stand breathing the same air as me, can you?' He wags his finger in front of my face. 'You can't even bear sleeping in the same bed as me.' His accusation hangs between us like a toxic cloud.

'You try sleeping in the same room with someone who's snoring, farting and stinking of drink.' Shit. The words are out before I can stop myself. I'm walking a fine line here, one which wavers between me knowing I need to stick up for myself, with one that needs to keep the peace. No matter what I say here, I'm not going to win.

However, *sometimes* sticking up for myself *does* win – if I catch him in the mood when he's feeling like any sign of strength in me means I might leave him. At these times, he'll often start bleating about how he doesn't want anyone else to have me. At other times, it just makes him angry. But me being a wimp and just accepting his crap seems to be the thing that *most* pushes him over the edge – it seems to make him despise me.

'You try being with someone who's frigid, boring and scared of her own shadow.'

Oh, so this is the way we're going today.

Maybe if we argue, Justin will slam out of the house like he would have done before this stupid pandemic. He might not have a pub to go to today, but surely someone, somewhere will sell him enough drink to knock himself out. Maybe I could lock the door and not let him back in.

'No Justin,' I retort. 'I'm *only* scared of *you* as it happens. I'm scared of what you might say, what you might do, how you make me feel.' He opens his mouth as though he's going to argue back but then closes it again. 'That's what you want, isn't it? To have this sort of control over me. And my kids *are* scared of you as well – *you're* the reason they're not here.' My voice is steady but carries the weight of regret. 'They've seen and heard enough, and your actions have driven them away. So if you want to know the *real* reason they're not here, there you have it.'

A heaviness settles in my chest as I struggle to get my breath back, the weight of my confession lingering in the tense atmosphere. I've said too much, I know I have, but seriously, what can he do to me? He's driven my kids away and he's already got me trapped here with him. He can't *physically* hurt me – not while I'm carrying his baby anyway.

Or maybe he can... His fingers whiten as his grip tightens around the bannister. 'What do you mean, *I'm* the real reason they're not here.'

'They've been telling Rick about you. About *us*.' My voice falters, my new-found fight somewhat ebbing. 'They feel safer there.'

'What the hell have you been saying about me?'

'It's not what *I've* been saying. It's what they've seen and heard for themselves.'

The expression on his face suggests it might be a good idea to change tack and steer the subject away from my children.

'What the hell's happened to you Justin? What did I ever do to deserve any of this? I thought things were getting better between us over the last week.'

He flies from the stairs and rushes at me.

20

'I'LL TELL you what you *did,* shall I?' He grabs my wrist as he faces me. 'What you always do – you stand there, in judgment, day after day, *you* - so holier than thou.' He shakes my arm around as he rants. 'While all the time, you're just sneaking around with your stashes of money and your secret plans.'

'What are you talking about?'

Oh my God, *what if he's found out about my money for the house?* But how could he have done?'

'If the kids are bad-mouthing me, it's because of *you.* You're turning them against me, just like Lynette did with Cameron. And if you think I'm going to let you do it with this one.' I wince as he jabs a finger from his free hand into my belly.

'Get away from me.'

But he continues to roar into my face. Not only will Diane be able to hear him two doors down, they'll probably be able to hear him on the other side of the square.

'It's *you* that's changed, not me,' he continues, now poking me in the chest so hard that he's certain to leave bruises. At least they can't be seen there, not like they can on my arms. 'Look at the bloody state of you – it's no wonder I can't stop drinking.' He grabs for my other wrist but misses. 'You need to take a long, hard look in the mirror.'

'Oww, you're hurting me.' I wriggle my arm around and somehow manage to wrench it from his grasp.

As I back away, he comes forward until I feel the hallway wall behind me. 'You've been bad-mouthing me to your ex, haven't you? What's going on there then?' This time he grabs my hoodie, a fistful of fabric in each hand as he slams me against the wall. 'Are you still sleeping with him, is that what this is?'

'No, please! Get off me.'

'How can I ever trust you, Melissa?' He lets go of my hoodie and grabs both my wrists, squeezing even tighter this time. 'How do I know that it's even MY kid you're carrying? I've got a good mind to pay that Rick a visit.'

Whiskey hangovers often cause him to wake up like this. With beer hangovers, he's more lethargic and just spends the day nursing a sore head. But a heavy night on the spirits seems to send him somewhere else entirely.

'Please just stop it, Justin. Why don't we calm down? I'm sure we can sort this out.' I've been like this since things soured between us at Christmas. Constantly trying to appease him. If only I'd packed us all up and left when his mask first slipped. Instead, I've been wavering and telling myself all sorts of stories that have stalled the only thing that I should have done.

The prospect of *sorting things out* must calm him for he releases my wrists. I edge away from him and into the kitchen. My heart's racing so fast, it feels like it could explode, and my throat's dry with fear.

As I'm filling a glass with water, I sense him behind me again.

I swing around. 'Why don't you go for a walk and clear your head?' His face is beetroot-red. It's another hot day but his colour is probably more down to rage and hangover.

'So you're trying to get rid of me now?' His eyes bulge and a vein throbs in his forehead. Another sign of his fury.

'Perhaps we could do with a bit of space from each other. We've been stuck like this for eleven days.'

Really, after what he said about *stashes of money,* I need to check my bank account – I must make sure my money's safe. I might also try that letting agent again. Perhaps the tenants have gone by now. I know they're not supposed to have done but I can live in hope.

'Is it so you can ring *him?*'

'Who?'

'Your ex-husband, who do you think I mean?'

'Of course not.'

'Show me your phone.' He holds the flat of his palm towards me.

'What for?' I rack my brains. I think I've deleted anything I wouldn't want him to see. Apart from my most recent message to Annie. If he sees that, he'll know my plans to leave him are still in full swing.

'I want to see your messages.'

That's what I was worried about. 'Actually, I need to wee.' I slip around the side of him, loading an urgency into my voice. 'You know what it's like when you're pregnant.'

'I said I want to see your phone. *Now.*' He slams his palm against the counter.

I turn in the doorway. 'It's upstairs. I'll bring it down with me.'

While in the bathroom, I slide my phone behind the bath panel. If he gets hold of it, he'll either take it from me or smash it, I'm certain of it. I wouldn't put anything past him, the mood he's got up in this morning, and without my phone, I'm as good as cut off from *everyone.* Somehow, I need to deflect his attention to something else.

I sit on the toilet for several minutes, frantically wiping at my tears. As fast as one drips from my chin, another slides down my face. The lump in my throat feels like I've swallowed a golf ball and right now, I wonder how I'll stop myself from crying so I can return downstairs. If Justin sees me like this, it'll only make him angrier.

As I descend the stairs, the familiar hiss of a beer can punctuates the air. Almost at the same time, there's a hammering at the door. Whoever's out there means business.

'Who is it?' I shout from behind the door, my voice still heavy with choked-back tears. Surely people shouldn't be calling at each other's houses with everything that's going on?

'It's the police.' A muffled voice calls back. 'We've had reports of a disturbance.'

I glance back to where Justin's now standing in the kitchen doorway. 'Get rid of them,' he hisses, his expression now wide-eyed and completely different to what it was a few minutes ago. 'Please Melissa. I'm sorry for grabbing you, truly I am. Please don't get me locked up – I can't take it, I really can't. Besides, I'll probably catch the virus if you let them chuck me in some cell at the police station.'

'We just need to make sure everything's OK in there?'

'It's all fine,' I call back, trying to steady my voice. 'Really it is.' I can tell from Justin's face that already, he's calmed down.

'We just need to make sure.'

This could be my big chance to make it out of here. I could open the door and tell them I need help. I could tell them that I want to leave but that I've got nowhere to go yet. However, if I did that, they'd have to take me *somewhere,* which would probably be to some women's hostel.

Everyone else would have their kids with them in a refuge – and I just wouldn't be able to bear being among them without my own two. Rick's hardly going to release my kids to me if I'm staying somewhere like that – and I wouldn't expect him to. Even I know they'd be better off with him in those circumstances. And what would happen to all our things if I did that?

'We just need to *see* you.' This police officer isn't going away.

Then, of course, there's the virus to think about. At least while I'm here, in this house, I'm not touching surfaces that other people have touched. I really do *not* want to catch it – who knows what it might do to me.

'You'll have to open up to them,' Justin hisses. 'Just make sure you leave the chain on.'

'Would you mind standing away from the door?' I slide the chain across and open the door a fraction. 'I'm pregnant and I'm asthmatic.'

'Right you are.' He steps back just as the edge of the door catches against the chain. He's got a look of Rick, with his unruly blonde hair and stocky build. The realisation brings fresh tears to my eyes. If only Rick hadn't begun his sordid affair with Cara. We could have still been together, instead of me being stuck in what's become a completely impossible situation.

'As you can see, I'm perfectly OK.'

He can probably tell I'm not. My face will still be blotchy and red from when I was crying, no doubt.

'We've received reports of a man shouting.' Concern is still etched across the officer's face. I evidently haven't yet convinced him.

'It might have been the TV they heard.' I try to force a laugh. 'My husband does have it on very loud.'

The look on the officer's face says, *do you expect me to believe that?* 'Is he in there with you? Your husband, I mean?'

I look back to the kitchen door where Justin's doing cut-throat signals.

'Erm, yes, but I think he's just on the phone at the moment. He's upstairs. Look, I promise you – everything's alright.'

The officer nods. 'And is there anyone else in there with you? Any children?'

His question brings me flat to the floor again. 'No,' I say quietly.

'OK. I'll leave you to it this time, but please don't hesitate to call us out if you need us.' He brings his hat up to his head as he nods at me in farewell. 'Anytime.'

'I will. And thank you.'

'Stay safe,' he adds as he lifts the latch on our gate.

I don't know whether he means from the virus or from my husband.

21

ONE OF THE reasons I'm up so early this morning is so I can check my bank account. Justin hardly let me out of his sight yesterday so I didn't end up checking it.

I've been lying awake since the sun rose, racking my brains about the day the country first went into lockdown and what I was doing on my computer. I remember finding that second property on one of the other estate agents' sites, then I logged into my savings account to check what money I had available. The next thing I recall was having to hurriedly close the screen when Justin suddenly appeared.

It must have been when I took the phone call from the letting agent that he re-opened my laptop and found my earlier email. I just hope and pray that my bank automatically logged me out of my account - I'm not sure how much time has to elapse before that happens.

I hover my fingers over the keyboard. The login is all pre-populated. Even if I *had* been logged out, he might *still* have been able to get back into it.

My heart's thumping as my account loads up. I scrunch my eyes together, trying to visualise the figures that show the funds I've so carefully saved since the turn of the year. The funds that will set me free and bring me and my children back together. I daren't look. What if he's...

He has.

The bastard.

The transaction was sent at 15:57 on Monday 26th March. £1532 to Justin L Rose. My balance is now zero. I had the first month's rent saved, the bond for the letting agent and the fee for the man with a van covered.

And now I've got absolutely nothing.

A searing anger twists in my gut, every muscle tensing at the realisation of what he's done. I want to pummel him with my fists, but I know it would only endanger both me and the baby. It won't matter what I do or say, I can't imagine any circumstances where he'd just turn around and give me it all back.

Somehow, I'll just have to replace the money, but with my job on pause, and still no sign of any of this so-called furlough money, I don't know how long that will take.

I stare at the zeros on the screen until they blur before my eyes. I hate him – I *hate* him. What could have ever made him think he had the right to steal my savings?

Perhaps I could get in touch with *my* bank – see if they'll reverse the transaction. But I know, deep down, I'd be wasting my time. I'm totally to blame for letting someone else get at my account.

I fight back tears, my mind a chaotic battleground of fear and regret. How could I have left my computer vulnerable? It was a costly oversight, a mistake I'll pay for dearly.

I slowly close the laptop lid – all fight seeping from me. It's not as if I have many options to replace that money. The first would be to get Justin to repay it, which isn't going to happen in a million years. The second is to hope and pray that work will pay me something soon, or thirdly, that the government will give us all something to live on. They've mentioned something in the news, but there's no sign of what or when that will be. They're all mouth and no trousers, as Mum would say.

Whatever they're planning to give to everyone will probably be just as they describe it, *something to live on.* Justin has already made a call about it but I don't know if, or when a payment is going to be made to us.

The third option is to get a loan lined up. I've thought of asking Rick but my pride gnaws at me. My two credit cards are already maxed out and I'm still paying back a loan I took when I needed things for the kids last year. Normally, my first port of call in this sort of situation would have been Mum. If only she'd realised the importance of appointing a power of attorney sooner, I'd probably have been able to borrow something from her estate. By the time I realised this would be necessary, she was already deemed to be without the appropriate capacity to sign the paperwork.

By then, I'd realised she was a danger to herself if she remained in her house, even with me and the carers checking up on her. Since she's gone into the care home, she's deteriorated fast. It wasn't long before she only recognised me and the kids on a good day - and just lately, this has become an *exceptionally* good day.

Her house money is tied up paying her care home fees and only after she dies, will I get the portion they're not allowed to use towards them. This is an awful way to think but sadly, it's become the reality.

I can't imagine any of the friends I work with having a grand and a half to spare, but Annie might have it. Simon's the one with all the money but she might be able to lay her hands on enough to help me.

I glance at the clock. If she's not on shift today, it's possibly too early to be texting her. But if she is, she'll be up and about, getting ready.

She envied me being sent home from work when I last saw her, but I envy her still having a degree of normality in her world. For having a familiar routine and a sense of being vital. She's what is classed as an *essential worker*. One that gets to go first in queues for the supermarket and receive their much-coveted home delivery slots. If we don't get one soon, I'm going to have to give in and ask Justin to go to the supermarket, with all the risk that brings.

> Morning hon - I'm sorry to text so early. xx

>> It's fine - I'm just getting ready for work. Sorry I didn't get back in touch the other day - it's manic. xx

> You don't have to apologise. How are you doing? xx

>> It's awful. Really awful. We had to sort some makeshift intensive care wards. I'm terrified I'm going to catch it myself but so far, I'm fine. Anyway, what's up – are you OK? And I forgot to ask in my last message – how are the kids? xx

> They're with their dad. Look I hate to ask you when everything's so difficult but I need your help. xx

>> What is it? And why are the kids with their dad? xx

> Long story. But it's fine – they're OK there. Anyway, Justin's found the money I'd saved up and he's taken it. All of it. xx

> You're joking!! I thought you had it stashed well away from him. xx

I hang my head. What an idiot I was to leave my computer logged in. Not only will Justin do *anything* to prevent me from leaving him but he's always desperate for cash. I've no idea what the scale of his debt is, but his alcohol addiction alone must cost him hundreds of pounds each month.

I don't think he's gotten anywhere with his pathetic blackmail attempt with Simon and he's also lost his job. I take a deep breath. I hate asking people for money but it's got to be done.

> I thought I had. Look, I know this is a big ask, but can you loan the money to me when these restrictions are lifted? So I can get into the house??? It's just until I get on my feet then I can pay you back?? xx

I drum my fingers against the kitchen table, my heart hammering inside my chest as I watch the three dots flashing on my phone screen for what feels like an eternity.

I'm as desperate to get away from Justin as he seems to be for me to stay. He was super-nice after what happened between us yesterday and after the police had gone, but I know only too well that it won't last. It never does.

Annie's reply slides onto my screen. In the same way, I was frightened to look at my account balance a few moments ago, I'm now almost too scared to read her reply.

> I'm really sorry hon. We're all in a similar boat. Simon's had to close the pub so our only income is my wage and what he'll get from that tenant in his old flat. But she's not able to work either so we could be waiting a while for her rent. I really am sorry. You know I'd help if I could. xx

She doesn't reiterate her offer from before for me to stay with them at the pub. But I guess she can't now. Who could ever have predicted that it would be against the law to stay with one of your friends when you're trapped in a toxic marriage?

Not that I'd go anyway. How could I? She can't help me so what am I going to do? My thoughts chase each other around for a few minutes until I hear movement overhead.

Justin's getting up.

Here we go again.

22

THE PILLOW beneath me is still soaked from my earlier tears. Glancing at the clock, I realise only an hour of respite has passed. I've never been one for daytime sleep, but exhaustion has driven me to the brink. Justin, thankfully, has let me be.

Staring at the ceiling, striped with sunlight, I try to drown out the distant lawnmower and children's laughter. I pull my pillow over my head, seeking solace in its comforting weight.

I usually love this time of year – when the clocks have gone forward and Easter is approaching. But right now, I can hardly bear to get back out of bed. Being here is a good excuse not to have to be in Justin's company and sleeping is a great way to kill some time – the days are endless beyond belief.

I'll move myself in time for the next daily briefing – when there might be a sliver of hope that the pandemic could be abating. When there's an end to all this. I know in my heart of hearts, this won't be coming yet, not with the death figures which I've been watching like a hawk. I've never felt as trapped in my life. If it was anything else, anything other than a virus that has the power to kill me and the baby, I'd be straight out of here.

'Ah, you're awake.' Justin appears at the door. 'You said to give you a call if you were more than an hour up here.'

'Did I?' I know full well that I didn't but I don't want to provoke an argument. Especially not while he seems to be in a decent mood for a change.

'So I've brought you some tea.' Justin's voice is gentle as he ducks under the doorframe and shuffles across the carpet towards me. In one hand, he's holding a steaming mug and in the other, a plastic bottle, looking as though it's filled with beer. God, I hope not - the last thing I need is him getting off his face yet again. I thought he'd finished up all the alcohol in the house.

His moods swing like a pendulum, erratic and unpredictable, a rollercoaster careering between the heights of neediness and the depths of unreasonable anger. Mum, if she were still compos mentis, would be horrified at the situation I'm in. She would have whipped me out of here faster than the virus is spreading.

But it's comforting, in a weird way, to sense Justin's weight as he sits beside me on our bed. I would never have put up with this kind of treatment before and keep wondering what's got into me. I hate the vulnerability that pregnancy has thrust upon me. Even the smallest crumbs of affection Justin offers feel like lifelines. Annie's warnings echo in my mind all the time and I wish I'd listened before escape became impossible. I long for her sharp words and offers of help but she's too busy at the hospital now.

In the past few days when we've messaged, she's told me about how the other nurses are dropping like flies after contracting the virus, and the double shifts she feels compelled to work as they're so short-staffed. She's often sleeping at the hospital between her shifts and says what they're coping with is harrowing. How can I possibly discuss my problems with her? My stuff pales into insignificance in comparison with what she's living through.

Justin's voice, heavy with concern, fills the room. 'Are you OK, Melissa?' His hand rests on my arm, the warmth of his touch a stark contrast to the chilly atmosphere that still lingers between us. 'You won't even look at me.'

I feel the weight of his words, but the bitterness lingers like the taste of the tea. I should confront him about the money but right now, I don't have the energy.

I pull the cover up to my neck. I stripped down to my bra and knickers before getting into bed and I don't want him to get any ideas.

'I'll sort everything – I promise. I'll change.'

I stare at his earnest face wrestling with wanting to say, *yeah, and how many times have I heard this now?*

'Anyway,' he continues. 'I also came up to tell you that Simon messaged while you were asleep.'

'He did? Saying what? Is Annie alright?' I can't help but worry about her. She's bound to catch the virus sooner or later and then, from everything I've heard, it's an utter lottery as to what it could do to her, or anyone else for that matter.

'He never mentioned her. But he's agreed to pay me the five grand as soon as he's able to reopen the pub. He's clearly desperate for me to keep his little secret.'

I stare at his face, lit up with the success of what he's achieved. I can't believe it. Or maybe I can. The question is, can I sit back and allow my husband to blackmail my friend's husband without doing anything?

'In the meantime...' He swigs from his bottle. 'He's got gallons upon gallons of beer to get rid of – I've already noticed him leaving bottles of it on the doorsteps of his regulars. The knowledge I've got about the stag do has been more lucrative than I could have ever imagined.'

'You're joking, aren't you?'

'So I've persuaded him to include me in his little arrangement from now on.' A smile spreads across his face. 'Not that he needed much persuasion with what I've got on him.'

'So you're going to be getting beer left here every day?'

He taps the side of his nose. 'He did say that he hopes it chokes me, but yes, all I have to do is make sure I leave him my empties.'

I prop myself up on my pillows and reach for my tea. 'How many empties?' Well, this is great – he's going to be drinking twenty-four-seven by the sounds of it.

'Oh, I don't know – just two or three bottles a day should keep me going. Don't worry – I promise I won't go mad.' He's grinning like a cat that's been given a saucer of milk. 'Like I told him, his beer is coming to a good home here and it's miles better than it being poured down a drain.'

'You said you were going to stop drinking.'

'Beer's fine. For God's sake, it's only barrel stuff. Anyone would think I was pouring top-shelf stuff down my neck every night, the way you carry on at me.'

I could remind him about the amount of whiskey he's consumed since we locked down, but instead, I close my eyes and lean back against the pillow.

'Anyway, I'm going to jump in the shower.' He stands from the bed. 'Do you fancy joining me?'

'No, you're alright. I'm just going to drink my tea.' I open my eyes and smile weakly. I can't think of anything worse than getting naked in the shower with him.

'You can save yourself for when I get back out then.' He places his bottle beside my cup and strides toward the ensuite. 'Like you promised.'

'When?'

'The other day. You said we needed to get close again.'

I want to shout after him that I said no such thing. Why on earth would I say something like that? *Or did I?* God, I feel like I'm going crazy at times. I've said things to keep the peace, I know I have, but surely I wouldn't have offered any hint that I want to have sex with him. The very thought turns my stomach.

As the shower starts running, I stare at his bottle for a few moments, resisting the urge to pour what's left of the beer out of the open window. As well as whatever's downstairs. I can hardly believe he's going to get daily beer delivered to the house. And surely Simon won't end up giving in to him and giving him five grand hush money? He's got grounds to go to the police with what Justin's doing to him.

But I know how much he loves Annie, despite what he might have done when egged on by drink and his friends. His proposal of marriage to her was incredible. With a couple of her work colleagues, she was skydiving to raise money for the neonatal unit at her hospital and Simon had gone to watch her. But unbeknown to her, and despite his lifelong fear of heights, he'd secretly booked his own skydive where he was planning to exit the plane at the same time as her. The video footage was awesome. I had tears in my eyes watching him in free fall with his *Will You Marry Me, Annie?* banner.

But I also know that Annie would be straight out of the door and would take him for far more than five grand when what he's done comes out.

Justin's out of the shower already. Damn, that was quick. I need to get out of this room sharpish. I swing my legs to the floor just as the ensuite door swings open. I reach towards the end of the bed for my dressing gown and drag it over my chest in an attempt to cover myself.

'Stay right where you are.' He whips the towel from his waist and drags it left and right across his back. 'I can't think of a better way to spend a Friday afternoon, can you?' He throws himself on the bed beside me just as I'm standing from it, reaching for my shoulder to tug me back. 'Seeing as you slept apart from me last night, *again,* we can make up for it now.'

'What do you mean?' I twist to look at him, though really, I know exactly what he means.

'It's about time we acted like we're married, don't you think?' He takes my chin in his fingers as he so often does when he wants something from me. 'I know you're a bit delicate at the moment so don't worry, I'll go easy on you.' He tugs at my dressing gown with his free hand.

He really thinks he's going to have sex with me. 'You know I'm not right at the moment. And I've still got the sickness.' I try to tug the dressing gown back. *Why, oh why didn't I get out of this bedroom the minute he got in the shower?*

'Don't give me that crap, Melissa.'

'It's not crap. You know I've been struggling.' I hold his gaze as if this will convince him that I'm telling the truth.

A darkness I've become all too familiar with creeps into his eyes. 'You're lying. You haven't thrown up the whole time we've been at home together.'

'How would you know? You've been drunk most of the time.'

He pushes against my shoulder as he tries to send me back against the pillows. 'Maybe I've been drinking because *you've* forced me to kill my sex drive.' He wags his finger in my face. 'Come on, Melissa.' His voice softens slightly and takes on more of a pleading edge. 'We've no kids here at the moment, neither of us has got to go to work – I don't know what your problem is.'

'My problem is that I'm four months pregnant and I don't feel like it.' I'm getting a vibe from him that I don't like. I feel vulnerable here. More vulnerable than I ever have. I'm suddenly fearful that he's going to just try and take what he wants from me.

'You're acting like we've been married for fifty years instead of for just one, Melissa. And you're acting as though you're seventy years old.'

I've got to get away from him. 'I'm just not in the mood right now.' I wriggle away but he grabs my leg and pulls me fully onto the bed. 'Get off me – what are you doing?'

'Come on. You know you want to.' His voice is leery, yet firm as he moves right up to me. I could be done for here. Maybe I should go through the motions. It's got to be better than him forcing himself onto me. Perhaps I can just allow him to get it over with and then he might leave me alone. But the thought of him lying on top of me, writhing around inside me really does make me feel physically sick.

As he manoeuvres himself up and over me, I try to squirm from beneath him.

'There is no part of me *whatsoever* that wants to have sex with you at this moment. Please leave me alone, Justin.' My voice is low and firm. 'You try anything and I'll—'

'I'm your fucking husband,' he roars. In one move he rises and sits fully astride me, his chest still glistening with water from the shower.

'Get the hell off me!' I cry as I thrash beneath him. I can't shake him off. 'You'll hurt the baby.'

'*You'll hurt the baby,*' he repeats, his voice full of scorn as he flops back to the side of me. 'That's all you seem to care about. There's something wrong with you, do you know that? You're fucking frigid. I think you should see a doctor.'

I hate that word. *Frigid.* But at least I've shaken him off. Relief floods me as I lean forward to get off the bed. But I'm not quick enough to prevent what comes next. His arm swings around and he grabs me squarely between my legs. 'No! Owww!' I screech as he squeezes at my crotch with all his might.

'You frigid bitch!' He bellows. 'Go on, fuck off out of here!'

I grapple on the bedside table for my asthma inhaler before scooping up my dressing gown from where it's landed on the floor. With tears blurring my vision, I stumble to the door.

He won't have hurt the baby with what he's just done.

But he's hurt me.

23

'WE'VE HAD reports of an altercation at this address.' A fresh-faced officer with kind eyes steps closer to the door. 'Are you Melissa Rose?'

Disbelief clenches my stomach as I grapple with the reality of their presence. I nod back, feeling the breeze on my face seeping through the gap between the door and the doorframe, my anxiety tightening with every passing second. 'Who called you?'

Whoever it is, I need to stop them. I don't want this extra threat of the virus that people coming to the door will bring.

'I'm sorry but I can't tell you that.' Her voice is soft and concerned. The sympathetic look in her eyes brings the all-too-familiar heat to my own.

'I'm PC Laura Fletcher,' she says, 'from North Yorkshire Police, and this,' she gestures to an equally youthful male officer standing at my gate, 'is PC Tom McDonald.' She turns back to me. 'Who's in the house with you?'

'Just my husband.' The word *husband*, once a source of warmth, now sticks in my throat, a bitter reminder of my shattered illusions. I steal a glance towards the top of the stairs, where Justin looms ominously, mouthing the words, *get rid of them* at me.

I turn back to the officer as she glances down at her notepad. 'That would be Justin Rose?'

'Yes.'

Shame wraps around me like a suffocating cloak. However, I can't tell her what's just happened. They'll cart Justin off to the police station, there's no doubt about it. And who knows how many other infected people will have been in the police car and the interview room before him? I can't risk him bringing the virus back to me. At least against Justin, I've got a chance of defending myself, but I've no idea what chance I might have against the virus.

'Does anyone else live here with you?' She steps closer as if trying to peer in. But I'm not letting this chain off the door.

'My children do, but they're staying with their dad at the moment.'

'Are you shielding, Melissa? Is that why you won't open the door?'

'I'm four months pregnant. And asthmatic,' I reply. 'So yes.'

'Right. Well, I'm not going to ask to come in but, I'd like you to step outside.' The tufts of her blonde hair poking from beneath her hat flutter in the breeze.

'I can't.'

'Just for a minute and I'll keep at a safe distance. PC McDonald,' she gestures to him again, 'will go around the back and speak, also at a safe distance, with your husband.' Her voice is authoritative but I just want them to go away.

'Why?'

'This is the second time we've been called to this address in a matter of days,' she remarks, her gaze unwavering. 'We need to be satisfied that everything's alright here.'

'Like I said, I'm shielding. I can't risk coming outside.' The chill of the metal chain against my palm matches the panic in my voice. She must come into contact with tons of different people every day. No way am I going anywhere near her.

'Like I said, we'll remain two metres away from you both. But we do need to see you properly. We have a duty of care to adhere to.'

'I'm fine, honestly, I am.'

'If I can just speak to you privately – out here, then I can see that for myself.'

Her insistence deepens the conflict within me; I'm torn between the fear of exposure to the virus and the need to protect myself from Justin.

'We have enough information from the report we've received to just take your husband in for questioning – regardless of what you do or say.'

'You have?' My voice is a squeak.

'When all this.' She waves her hand in the air. 'Could be ironed out by the two of you cooperating with myself and my colleague.'

'Just a second please.'

With a resigned sigh, I close the door to release the chain. Justin arrives at the bottom of the stairs. 'Watch what you say to them,' he hisses.

His tone is so low, I can't tell whether his voice contains fear at the possible comeuppance that could be in store for him, or a threat towards me if I were to tell the police the truth about how he's been behaving.

'OK, I'll step right back to the gate,' PC Fletcher says as I open the door. 'Is your husband going to the back door to speak with my colleague?'

I check over my shoulder. 'Yes.'

I wait for her to move away before shuffling onto the porch. Several neighbours are out watching from the other side of the street. Part of me feels like yelling at them to bugger off inside but that's only going to draw even more attention to us.

They've all got a ringside view from where they are, especially the two neighbours who are immediately opposite. We'll have to keep our voices right down to ensure they won't be able to hear anything of our conversation. I can hardly bear to consider what they must all be thinking of me.

My attention's averted to the new neighbour and to Monica, who was asking if I was alright only this morning. I guess she has her answer now.

'We've received a report of a man shouting and being abusive – your husband, I take it?'

I step off the porch and onto the garden path. I *really* don't want our spectators to hear what I'm saying. 'We've argued, yes, but it's all sorted out now.'

'We've been told of you being heard shouting, *get off me,* and evidently in some distress.' She leans forward onto the gate while not taking her eyes off me. 'Tell me what's happened in there, Melissa.'

'It's all fine, honestly, it is.' My face is on fire.

'But, it's not fine, is it? And you don't have to put up with being treated like this. We can help you, if you'll let us.'

I stare back at her. Her idea of help will be to chuck me into some women's refuge. I couldn't bear it in normal times, but at a time when I might catch something that could kill me and the baby, the prospect of a refuge is unthinkable.

I've seen the pictures on the news of those who've caught the virus and heard about them from Annie. Many of them are on ventilators. And they're fast running out of them. People are struggling to breathe, abandoned in hospital corridors because there aren't enough beds. No matter how awful things are between me and Justin, I'm definitely safer staying here until this is over.

'How did you get those bruises on your arms?' PC Fletcher's voice is gentler than in the whole time since she arrived.

24

'WHAT BRUISES?' Though I know exactly what she's asking about. *Shit.* Why didn't I put my cardigan on before answering the door?

'Has your husband been hurting you, Melissa?' She keeps her voice low. Hopefully, no one other than me can hear what she's saying. 'Because if he has, we can arrest him for assault. We can protect you from him.'

'I bruise easily, that's all.' My voice is a mumble. 'I'll have knocked myself while I've been spring cleaning. I've been trying to keep myself busy.'

Justin's elevated voice echoes from around the back, although I can't make out what he's saying.

PC Fletcher frowns at me. I can tell what must be going through her mind. I might as well have told her *I walked into a door.* Really, I want to let her know that I'm not stupid and that I'm planning to leave here as soon as it's safe and I've been able to recoup the money I need.

If I can manage to keep the peace with Justin until then, I can get through this. It can't be too hard. I know what annoys him and similarly, I know how to get around him. No matter what, he definitely still loves me on some level, so as long as that remains the case, I've got some leverage.

'I'm going to leave this card on your wall, OK?' PC Fletcher says.

'What is it?'

'It's a domestic abuse helpline.' She scribbles on it. 'I'm also leaving you my name and number. If you need any help, you call me. But if it's an emergency, obviously call the three nines. This and any other calls we've attended here will be logged, so we'll be straight out to you.'

'Honestly, it was just a row – I'll be fine.'

'Please just take the card. Keep it somewhere safe, and remember you're not on your own here. As soon as you feel able and ready, we can help you, I promise.'

My nod back at her is tight, the lump in my throat stifling any words.

'I'm going to stand by the car but I'm not getting back into it until you've put this card in your pocket.'

I know she means well, but I'm exhausted with it all. If it wasn't for the virus, I probably *would* press charges for what he did to me upstairs, but right now, I feel too weary and weak. I don't know what I want to do the most, sleep or cry.

I peer from behind the curtain as the police car eventually disappears around the corner by the pub, and the neighbours return to their houses and back gardens.

'I need more beer.' Justin drains his bottle and heads out of the lounge. 'And I want to know who involved the police again. If I find out it was *you*—'

'They'll have heard you shouting when we were upstairs.' I follow him into the kitchen.

'I can't believe the fucking neighbours we've got. They're a set of nosy bastards. They've nothing better to do with their sad little lives.'

'You really hurt me before.'

Maybe I got off lightly with him just squeezing my groin as he did. There was a moment when I feared he was going to force himself on me.

'When I find out who's making those calls.' He swings the fridge door open with the force of a storm. 'They're going to wish they'd never bloody met me.' He yanks a bottle from inside the door. 'I'll tell you what it is, shall I?' He turns on his heel, to face me, his eyes still flashing with anger.

'What?'

'It's that bitch of an ex-wife.'

'What's she got to do with any—?'

'She didn't only poison Cameron against me – she did it with the neighbours too.' He points in the direction of the square. 'With her lies and her accusations. This is all *her* doing.'

'No Justin.' I fight to keep my voice steady. 'The police coming to our door is all *your* doing. The windows were wide open. The neighbours were bound to have heard you. If I heard a neighbour screaming *get off me* and a man shouting at her, I'd probably call the police as well.'

He swigs from his bottle and I wait for him to swallow. I also wait for him to either accept what I've just said or for him to explode. His moods are like a nasty game of chance – and I'm always waiting to find out which one's going to hit me next.

Yet, I don't think he'll do anything to me *now*. Not *immediately* after the police have just been here – he wouldn't dare. He seems more concerned with what the neighbours think and what they might be saying to each other about us. He probably cares more about their opinions of him than he does about mine.

I flinch as he steps towards me. 'I do appreciate that you decided not to throw me under the bus before.'

Every part of me recoils as he gets so close that I get a whiff of the beer on his breath. I might not have wanted one of us carted off to where we might catch something, but the last thing I want is to be in his proximity.

'And I'm sorry about how I behaved upstairs,' he adds.

Blimey – he's apologising. I never expected this.

'However, you need to sort it out, you know.'

'*I* need to sort it out?' I step back from him and point towards myself. 'What do you mean?'

'I didn't get married to be forced to live a sexless existence, you know.'

Our eyes lock. How he thinks I could go *anywhere* near him, especially after how he grabbed me upstairs, is anyone's guess. Yet I need to be careful how I answer.

'I know we need to sort it out,' I find myself replying. 'And as soon I'm over all this feeling sickly, we'll be fine.'

Really, I'm just trying to buy myself some time.

25

THE CALENDAR MOCKS me with its repetition—day twenty of waking up to the same routine.

Justin is still in bed, a prisoner of his excesses. His drinking seems to be a testament to his deeper turmoil, one that I struggle to work out. What demons are driving him to consume alcohol to the extent he does?

For the first time since I've known him, the amount of alcohol he must have consumed yesterday made him violently sick last night. He sounded so ill, I almost felt sorry for him. *Almost.* At least this gave me a good reason to sleep in Aisla's room again and leave him to it.

He didn't bother me once.

I carry my tea to the front porch which is bathed in the morning sunlight. Gingerly lowering myself onto the wall, the warmth of the day contrasts sharply with the ache still enduring between my legs, a reminder of when Justin grabbed me. He couldn't have been sorrier straight after he'd done it, but that's beside the point.

Despite how ill he was before heading for bed, his rinsed-out plastic bottles are waiting on our porch all ready for Simon to refill.

I don't know what I *can* do other than to wait things out. After all, people have been fined for breaking lockdown rules, so I'm well and truly stuck here. It's not as if I've even got money to pay any fines with.

I stretch my legs out in front of me wondering what people would think and say if they knew of the bruising concealed by my baggy shorts. I can no longer wear my regular clothes – weight has dropped from me but my belly is certainly swelling.

Once again, the air is filled with birdsong. I look up at the trees dotted around the green, all laden with beautiful fragrant blossom. It should be such a wonderful place to live. I adored this house when I first saw it. I loved everything from its Georgian-style front porch to the *dancing lights* in the kitchen, as Aisla called them when the four of us were all dancing around in there shortly after we'd moved in.

As I gaze at the blooming daffodils and the promise of tulips, a fleeting wish flits through my mind. If only I could transplant this garden to the next chapter of my life. The flowers will change, but I hope that, by the time the tulips bloom, I'll have escaped the confines of this house.

All is quiet apart from the distant noise of what sounds like a hoover. I've never known the usually vibrant square so still. The usual football games on the green, the distant church bells, and the aeroplane activity from Leeds Bradford airport are all eerily absent. Once, in my former life, I might have enjoyed this space and this step back from reality. But as things stand for me, I hate it.

I tilt my phone toward my face and begin scrolling through the headlines. The fatality figures are getting scarier by the day and the media is speculating that we'll be kept inside our houses for longer than these initial three weeks. Tomorrow, we'll find out for certain but until then, I can continue to hope for a reprieve.

My attention is caught by three of the neighbours calling across from their gates to each other. The new neighbour is talking to Monica and someone who lives to Monica's right – someone who's never spoken to me. Diane told me she was friendly with Lynette, so that's probably why. They're close enough for me to hear the odd word, but not to gain the gist of their conversation. Then, as if they can sense me watching them, they all turn, firstly in my direction, and then to look at each other, their conversation suddenly halted. I'd go as far as to say they look uncomfortable.

'How are you doing Melissa?' The note of concern in Monica's voice reaches across our divide. The new lady scuttles to the door of her block of flats, her blonde hair flowing out behind her. She's a strange one. I've noticed her staring at the house and appearing to be watching me more times than I can remember since we went into lockdown. Yet now she has an opportunity to say something to me, perhaps to divulge the reason why she seems to be so interested in what I might be doing, she doesn't take it, and vanishes inside instead.

Perhaps I should cut her some slack. Perhaps she feels awkward, with her being new around here, or maybe she's just worried about making things worse for me. The neighbours on this side of the green would have to be continually blindfolded and wearing earplugs not to have realised what's been going on at our house.

I nod back at the two remaining women, wary of speaking in case Justin hears me. Our bedroom window is around the back of the house and he'd no doubt be down here like a shot if he were to hear me talking to the neighbours.

'Listen, love,' Monica says. 'I know it's none of my business but if you need help, you just ask for it, right.' She points at herself with the hand that's not holding a mug. 'I'm in the Facebook group – and I've noticed you're in it too.' She's dressed in cut-off jeans and a vest top and I bet she's happy inside her house – she's metres away from me, yet a million miles in terms of how different our lives probably are.

I put my finger to my lips as I nod back at her, while gesturing upwards. Given how ill Justin was last night, I imagine he'll be letting some fresh air into the room this morning, so will have the bedroom window wide open.

And aside from this, it's still so hot. The days are gloriously sunny from beginning to end. This will be a gift to those with beautiful gardens to tend to, or for children with their paddling pools. It's a stark contrast to the heavy emptiness I'm facing, day after day, separated from my children and uncertain of the future beyond this lockdown.

'I'm so sorry.' Monica lowers her voice. 'But listen to me. If you need *anything,* anything at all, just drop me a message on Facebook, won't you?'

How about one-and-a-half grand, I could reply. Though even if I had it in my back pocket right now, there's nothing I could do with it.

So I just nod back at her. 'Thanks,' I say, in a voice so small she probably doesn't even hear me.

26

FACETIME CALL - RICK MASON CALLING.

I prod at the green button while pushing my hair out of my face. There, the gorgeous faces of my children fill the screen and their joyous voices flood the air, the most wonderful sound I've heard all week.

'Mum!' Aisla gasps.

'Oh my God, I've missed you two.' I'm so excited to see them that I forget to lower my voice. I sink to my usual spot on the wall in the back garden, having moved myself out of sight of the main street. After Monica had finished speaking to me, another of the neighbours passed by, and while she only called 'hello' to me, her face was so filled with sympathy that it made my cheeks burn.

I raise the screen so it's level with my face. It's been nearly a week since I last clapped my eyes on them. 'How are you both?'

'We're OK,' Ewan replies. 'Apart from having to do so much *schoolwork*.' He pulls a face.

'We've got this screen thing called Zoom now,' Aisla adds. 'Where our teachers can talk to us from their own houses.'

'Just like we're talking to you now,' Ewan says, smiling. 'I've missed you, Mum.'

'You too sweetheart – both of you... and yes, I've heard of Zoom. I've spoken to Nana on it a couple of times.'

'I want to talk to Nana too.' Aisla pouts.

'You'll be able to very soon. Anyway, how's this schoolwork of yours going?'

'Oh-kay.' It's Ewan's turn to pull a face. Seeing them both is so wonderful that my current angst almost fades away for a moment.

'Does your dad know you're on his phone?' My face creases into a frown at the absurdity of my question. As if my children should need his permission to speak to me. I've been trying almost daily over the last few days to speak to them but Rick hasn't been picking up, and every message I've sent has been met with a curt response. I'll be having it out with him when all this is over, that's for certain.

'Yes. He's here. Say hello.' Aisla points the phone in his direction.

Rick, clad in saggy joggers and a baggy t-shirt, dismisses the phone with a furrowed brow, his unkempt hair begging for a cut. His appearance could be why he doesn't want to meet with me on screen. Or it could be something else, who knows?

'I got upset for you last night, Mum.' Aisla's smile fades.

'Are you and the baby alright?' Ewan adds with a seriousness that should be reserved for someone well beyond his years. A surge of guilt claws at my insides. Rick was right; my ten-year-old boy should not be worrying about me. 'We're good love. I've been—'

A shadow looms over me. Slowly, I raise my eyes to Justin. With a face like thunder, he plucks my phone from my hand. He slams his finger on the leave call button, cutting off my line to my children. Then he slides the side button to turn my phone completely off.

'Hey – what are you doing?' I jump up from the wall in an attempt to grab it back from him. However, as he storms back toward the house, he slides it into the pocket of his jeans. 'I was talking to my kids.'

'What did he mean, *are you and the baby alright?*'

I rush after him. 'Nothing! Nothing at all. He was only asking a question.'

'What does everyone think - that I'm some kind of monster?' Frustration taints his words. 'What the hell have you been telling them?'

I can only watch in horror as he directs his anger at the fridge, the metallic thud as his head connects with it, reverberating around us and leaving a new dent beside the one from January.

'You had no right taking my phone like that – I want it back.' I outstretch my hand.

'Oh you do, do you? What, just so you can rub my nose in everything?' He strides to where I'm hovering near the door and kicks it shut with his foot. Then he comes towards me.

'What are you on about?' I flatten myself against the wall.

He brings his face close to mine. 'You know *full well* Cameron told me where to go, don't you? That he won't even answer the phone to me?'

'What's that got to do with—?'

'What is it? Are you trying to prove who's the *better* parent?' He drives his finger into the wall at the side of my head as he continues to glare at me. '*Look at me – my kids still want to know me.*'

'Of course not. Please, Justin. Please calm down.' I duck under his arm and emerge by his side, poised to run to another room to escape him. I couldn't call the police for help even if I wanted to. He's got my bloody phone. But one of the neighbours probably will if he gets much louder.

He comes up behind me as I dither over where to go and what to do. His fingers close around the back of my neck, a sharp jolt of pain radiating through me as I try to pull away. 'So tell me then? What *are* you playing at?'

'I don't know what you mean.'

'The cosy conversations you've been having with your ex-husband behind my back?' I put my arm up to the counter to protect my belly as he pushes me toward it.

'*Behind your back?* You're being ridiculous. The kids are missing me, that's all. I wasn't even speaking to Rick.'

'*The kids are missing me.*' His voice is cold and mocking. 'Unlike *my* kid, you mean? You'll do *anything* to make me feel like shit, won't you?' He slams his fist onto the counter as he emphasises the word *anything*. 'Does it make you happy, rubbing my nose in it all?'

He loosens his grip on my neck, enough for me to be able to turn and face him.

'I'm not trying to make you feel like *anything*.'

All I care about right now is him calming down and letting me call the kids back. They'll be wondering what's going on. Ewan will be worrying. I'll run to the centre of the green if that's what it takes to get some space from him. Virus or no virus. 'Please, just give me my phone back Justin, if I can ring them back now, I can just pretend my battery died.'

'You can have it back after I've been to the chemist,' he says. 'I don't trust you to have it while I'm gone. How do I know you're not talking to *him?*'

'I thought we weren't going out anywhere.' I stare back at him. 'We agreed it's best for me if we don't go near other people.'

I need my inhaler. Stress always makes me breathless. I pull the drawer where I keep my spare open and rummage around for it.

'I need something for my stomach.' He sinks to a stool at the breakfast bar and drops his head into his hands. 'I'm still not feeling great. It's probably why I'm so cranky. Look, I'm sorry.' He looks up at me as though actively seeking my forgiveness.

Cranky. That's one word for it. His half-baked apologies can't possibly make up for how he's treated me, but I'll swap being grovelled to from being attacked and pushed around any day of the week. Thank God he's calmed down.

I breathe in the vapour of my inhaler, feeling instantly better. It's a taste and smell that's familiar and grounding, after all, I've been taking the drug for most of my life. *Familiarity* and *grounding* are exactly what I need right now.

'I do understand you're not well.' It's the biggest lie I've ever told. I might as well give him an open-ended invitation to push me around to his heart's content. But this is damage limitation. At least, my kids are well away from him and before this little one comes along, we'll be well away from him too.

'I can't go on like this. It's killing me.'

'Listen if you *must* go to the chemist, will you *promise me* you'll keep away from other people.'

'I'll wrap a scarf around my face,' he replies. 'My stomach's been rotten enough without me catching the virus on top of it. I feel like it would finish me off.' He rubs his stomach and pulls a face.

'Will you wash your hands as soon as you come back in?' I nod towards the sink. I just need to get him to leave my phone behind so I can call the kids back. 'And put your clothes straight into the washing machine. I'll bring a change down here for you while you're gone.'

'I'm sick of this bloody virus shit.'

'I need to ring Mum at the care home.' I keep my voice light. I can't believe I'm having to literally beg for my phone back from him. 'I promised I'd call her again today.'

'Well, bully for you. Who've I got to talk to?' He sounds pathetic. I've got no idea what must be going on in his head.

'You've got me, of course.'

'That's what I thought. But you seem to be going colder and colder on me.'

Oh God, he's back in needy mode. Still, I can handle this - it's the angry and aggressive side I've got little chance against. 'I'm just, you know, with this virus stuff and the baby and missing the kids – I'm not myself.'

'You're not the only one. You've no idea how much losing Cameron has affected me.' He rocks his head from side to side in his hands and I notice how the hair on top of his head is thinning far quicker than he'd like it to. 'Particularly when he's been turned so badly against me. It's not right, you must agree with that, surely?'

Discussing Cameron only ever winds Justin up, so I need to change the subject. 'Let's just get through whatever's left of this lockdown, shall we? Everything will be alright once we get back to normal.'

'Do you promise that you're not still planning to leave me?' Something in his face softens as he stands from the stool and walks back over to me. Maybe he *will* give me my phone after all.

'No, I'm *not* planning to leave you.' I should have my fingers crossed behind my back.

'I need you Melissa – I really do.' Beneath the words, there's a hint of possessiveness that sends shivers down my spine. He reaches for me and presses me into him. Once upon a time, a gesture like this would have made me melt, but these days I just stiffen and long to get away from him. His chin is stubbly and his breath smells dreadful. 'I need you and the baby. I even need Aisla and Ewan. I just want things to be back as they were and for us to be a happy family.'

'I know.' He can't see my face as I burrow my nose into his shoulder to escape the stench. Being so close to him is awful but I'm in survival mode here. Somehow, I'm going to raise the money again to leave him.

I have to bide my time and plan to get away from here meticulously. Aisla and Ewan are safe.

But me and this baby aren't.

27

'YOU'RE DOING yourself no favours, staying glued to that thing,' Justin nods at the TV as I watch the latest daily briefing.

I look from the screen to him as he sits on the armchair opposite me. 'As if the *prime minister* is in intensive care. I just can't believe it, can you?'

'So what? He's just another human being. What makes *him* so special? If you ask me, you're becoming obsessed with it all.' He's still wearing the same stained t-shirt from before he left for the chemist, and is clutching two plastic bottles of beer, which are presumably his latest doorstep delivery. I can understand Simon not wanting to pour his beer down the drain but I'm still shocked at him donating to Justin after his blackmail attempt. He must be *really* desperate to get rid of it.

'It's consuming everyone.' I roll my eyes before returning my attention to the TV screen, anticipation building for the next announcement. Shortly, we'll find out if we're going to be let out or continue to be trapped inside our houses.

'They're such brave souls, all those nurses who are facing the virus like they are. There's going to be a clapping again for them this week – if we're still in lockdown.'

'Well, like I said to you before – we're not getting involved in any of that crap.' He shakes his head.

I stare back at him. *How did I never see what he was really like before?* He's so heartless that he's trying to prevent me from publicly applauding the NHS. 'Well, *I'm* getting involved.'

'Why? It's not as if *you're* directly affected.' He leans forward in his chair.

'Annie's one of those nurses actually.'

'Oh yes, your best buddy.' He's always so sarcastic when I speak warmly about anyone else. 'I forgot about her.'

'Don't be like that. She's putting her life on the line every time she goes to work, isn't she?'

I follow Justin's gaze to the window as he suddenly jerks his head to face it. 'What's *she* bloody looking at.'

Diane strolls past, her curious gaze briefly meeting mine. I find comfort in the acknowledgement, especially since she's one of the few familiar faces in this square.

'I bet it was *her* who's been squealing to the police,' he says as she disappears around the corner.

'It could have been the *new* neighbour.' I avert my eyes to the flat window in the overlooking block. There the woman is, with her chin resting on her hands, watching us yet again. 'She doesn't seem to have a right lot else to occupy herself with.'

'Didn't I tell you to keep these curtains closed?' He lurches from the chair to the window and wrenches the curtains together.

'But it's such a lovely day,' I protest. 'Besides, I'm just as bad for being nosy. You know how much I love looking into windows as I'm walking by houses.'

His face relaxes into what might pass for a smile. I must have said the right thing for a change. I suppose I made a comment that binds the two of us together. I'm suddenly transported back to a time when I said things such as, *I'd like some wallpaper like that for our house,* or *our lounge is going to be as cosy as theirs when we move in together.*

This might be the best time, if there is such a thing, to delicately broach the subject of my missing money. I'm going to have to mention it sooner or later, and because of the moods he's been in, I've been putting it off and putting it off. So I take a deep breath. 'I need to ask you about something, Justin.'

'What now?' He folds his arms across his chest. He's defensive before I even say a word. He must be able to sense from my tone that I'm about to accuse him of something.

'The money in my savings account.'

There isn't a flicker of emotion in his face as he stares back at me. 'Aren't we a married couple?'

'Well yes, but–' At least he's not attempting to deny it. Not that he could – the transaction is there in black and white.

'So you've got no reason to be keeping money to yourself – especially with things as they are right now.'

'But that money—' I swallow. 'I need things for the kids – you can't just empty my account.'

He laughs. 'Well as you've found—'

'I need it back, Justin.' My voice wavers, desperation creeping in.

He remains unmoved. 'We need to conserve everything we've got until we know where there's some more money coming from.'

'Look – how about you just keep a few hundred of it and let me have the rest back in my account?' I can tell by his face that I'm wasting my breath. 'Honestly Justin, I had plans for it.' *Like somewhere else to live.*

'What does it matter? You're not exactly able to do anything right now, are you? But the bills still need paying and we have to eat.'

I resist the urge to say, *and you have to drink.* 'It matters because it's *my* money. I wouldn't just help myself from *your* bank account.'

'You'd have a job doing that right now.' His sarcastic laugh sends my fury soaring. How I'd love to wipe that grin off his face. No wonder his ex-wife hates him so much. He put on a good show for me though. And managed to keep it going for long enough to now have this power.

'Listen,' he says. 'I'll do a far better job than you of making what we've got last.'

Deep down, he must know the real reason for my secret money. He saw my email to the letting agent on the day we went into lockdown. But thankfully, that's a subject he doesn't seem to be opening up.

'Anyway.' He looks at himself in front of the mirror next to the window. 'I'm going to get myself out of here for another hour, I think.'

'But I thought— Since when? Where are you going?'

'I need some fresh air.' Then noticing my face, he adds. 'Like I said before, you're becoming obsessed with the whole thing. I'm beginning to think that both of us catching the virus might be a good thing in the long run.'

'How can you say that?' I study his face for a sign that he's joking. He's not. 'Are you mad?'

'I reckon most of what's been said in the news is to keep us under control in our homes. It's probably some sort of government propaganda.'

'Don't be stupid – of course it's not. Justin – people are dying out there. Dying in agony.' I bring my hand to my chest as though to comfort myself. Somehow, what he's saying could be a veiled threat to infect me. 'Surely you don't want to add me and the baby to that list.'

'I'm sick of hearing you say crap like that – if you catch it, you'll be fine. Lots of people get over it.'

'You can't say that.' I thought I was safe here. Safe from the virus, anyway.

'Bloody hell.' He throws himself back into the chair.

'Look, you've been to the chemist. If you keep going outside, we're asking for trouble.'

He shakes his head. 'It's a good job I'm getting that beer dropped off every day – to stave off the misery if nothing else.'

'What do you mean?' Like I need an explanation. It's another one of Justin's put-downs.

'I want you to start thinking and talking about something other than bloody Coronavirus. You're getting more and more boring by the day.' He jumps up again. 'In fact, no! I'm going out and you're not going to stop me.'

'Please promise me you'll stay away from other people – please Justin?' I jump up too and follow him through to the kitchen. 'For the baby's sake, if not for mine.'

'It's a real shame you can't come with me.' He pauses and looks at me.

I study his face, wondering if he's trying to be nice. Then he smirks and I realise that he's just trying to rub my nose in the fact that I'm a complete prisoner within these four walls. An hour's exercise each day and trips to the supermarket are luxuries that haven't been extended to me.

'It'd do you good to get out, wouldn't it? Oh well, never mind. What are you going to do while I'm gone?' He reaches for the watch I bought him the first Christmas we were together and snaps it onto his wrist.

'I'll just sit in the garden with my book.'

'You can wait until I'm back to do that.'

'Why?' Hell, he's even trying to control where I sit now.

'Because of how the neighbours have been carrying on.' He rises from the stool. 'I'd just like us to keep ourselves to ourselves as much as possible at the moment.' He slides his feet into the trainers he's left at the back door. 'We'll sit out there *together* when I've been for my walk.'

'You're certainly looking better than you did.'

'It's the prospect of getting out of here that's done it.'

'Will you shower and put all your clothes in the wash again when you get back?'

'I really think you're going over the top with that. But yes, if it stops you going on.'

'What about my phone? You said I could have it back.'

'After my walk.'

'Why can't you trust me? I'm only calling the kids.'

'After what I found on your computer – you're asking me to trust you?' He shakes his head. 'I don't think so.'

'You've taken everything from me. My money and now my phone.' The realisation hits hard, the weight of my helplessness settling in.

'I don't want to talk about this. I'll see you when I get back.'

He knows my fear of the virus, and yet, he's deliberately pushing me to the edge. How did I end up here, trapped and powerless?

The door bangs behind him. He knows exactly what he's doing.

28

As I HEAD BACK to the lounge, a woman's raised voice from outside prompts me to head straight to the window and peer around the curtain. The window's closed so I can't make out what she's saying but I'm just in time to catch the reply as I push the window ajar. *I might have bloody known.* It's the new neighbour and *Justin.*

She must be having a go at him about the money he's swindled. 'Just get lost and leave me alone.' He roars at her over the top of her gate. 'Or you'll fucking regret it.' He might not be directing his venom at me this time but just hearing the anger in his voice causes the hairs on the back of my neck to rise. She disappears inside and slams the door which is a relief. I'd hate for yet another person to find out the hard way what he's capable of.

My heart is thudding in my chest as he walks on. His leaving is risky in terms of bringing the virus back with him, but I can't deny that it provides respite for me, albeit briefly.

As my breath returns to normal, an unsettling calm cloaks the house, prompting a sudden urgency within me. This is as good a time as any for me to Facetime the care home to speak to Mum. I can get the headlines from this daily briefing anytime.

I dash into the kitchen and slide my laptop from the drawer.

Just as it's loading up, there's a knock at the door. Sighing, I stand from my chair and head to answer it.

This time I don't keep the chain on but call out that I'm shielding as I open the door.

'Melissa Rose?' A young lad asks, looking as though he's buckling under the weight of a box laden with fruit and vegetables.

'Yes, but I haven't ordered anything.'

'Well, someone has,' he retorts, his voice sharp, tossing the words over his shoulder as he unloads another crate, each thud echoing my rising anxiety.

'Who?'

He pulls a device from his pocket and taps a couple of buttons. 'I don't have the cardholder details but it's definitely for this address.' He glances towards my front door, as though making absolutely certain.

'It must have been my husband then.'

I'll be so glad when I don't have to use this phrase anymore. When *my husband* becomes *my ex*.

It takes me far longer than it normally would to get everything inside and into the kitchen as I daren't pick up a full box and risk straining my belly, nor can I ask the driver to carry anything inside for me. With the current pandemic restrictions, he isn't allowed to anyway.

This is typical Justin – he orders a delivery and then leaves it for me to bring it all in. Although I should perhaps be grateful that he's used the money he syphoned from my account for something other than alcohol.

It's weird though. The food is from a supermarket we wouldn't normally use and it's all branded stuff. Normally, we go for the supermarket's own options. However, it's been in the news that most people are struggling to get a delivery slot, so maybe that's the explanation. In addition to that, those who *can* go to the supermarket are stripping the shelves. So maybe he's just had to order whatever's available.

He hasn't ordered any more drink, which is baffling. I can only assume he placed the order while he was spinning his yarn about *not drinking ever again.*

I pile it all up beside the draining board, so it's ready to spray down and wipe after I've made the video call to Mum. Time's ticking by and I want to have my call with her before Justin gets back and tries to spoil it.

I take the empty boxes back to the front of the house, wash my hands and then settle back down in front of my computer at the kitchen table.

'Hi Melissa, it's lovely to see your face,' Sue, the home manager beams into the camera. 'How are you doing? How are the kids?'

'Oh, erm – we're all good thanks.' My voice echoes in the silence of the kitchen. How can I tell her the truth? How can I tell *anyone* the truth? That I'm trapped in a house with an abusive drunk, that my ex-husband won't allow my kids to come home and that I'm utterly powerless to do *anything* about any of it.

'Your mum will be so pleased to speak to you.' Sue stands from her office chair. 'I'll walk you through to her room. Just let me get a face mask on first.'

'At least you've managed to get hold of some.' I listen as she opens and closes the drawers in her desk. I know she'll be up against everything, working in the kind of environment she's in, but in a similar way to how I envied Annie back at the start of all this, I envy Sue too. She's doing something worthwhile and has a reason to get out of bed every morning. Meanwhile, what am I doing that's making a difference? Not a right lot.

'They're a supply we already had,' she replies, her voice now muffled behind the mask as she bends to pick up her laptop. 'We need to conserve them – we don't seem to be able to get hold of more anytime soon.'

'Does Mum have to stay in her room all the time?'

'Unfortunately, yes.' All I can see is the bottom of Sue's mask bobbing up and down at the top of my screen as she makes her way along the corridor. 'All the residents are staying in their rooms - they have to for their own safety. They've each got a designated member of staff looking after them as well. To minimise the risk of infection.'

A vision of Mum in her four walls enters my mind. Yes, I made those four walls nice for her with family photos and her most treasured items from her former home, but having to stay in one room is hardcore. It's difficult enough to stay in one house.

'It must be tough for you all. Have you had any virus cases there?'

'No – thank goodness. But our sister home has – it sounds like a total nightmare for them. Anyway, here we are. I'll pop the computer in front of her and then I'll leave you to speak for as long as you need.'

'Thanks, Sue.' I clear my throat as the weathered face of my darling mother appears on the screen. Her hair needs styling and her face is devoid of any makeup. Normally, I'm strict about her appearance being well-maintained.

'Hi, Mum.' I elevate my voice, attempting lightness, hoping she doesn't detect the tremor of my unshed tears.

Before Alzheimer's left her stuck in that wretched chair within those four walls, Mum would *never* go out without her hair curled and her pink lippy on. However, it sounds as if the staff are only able to take care of the resident's more basic needs right now. So there's little point in me complaining. I know I should just be grateful that she's being looked after and that she seems to be safe. The idea of my frail mum catching that awful virus terrifies me.

'It's so good to see you, Mum.' I greet her through the pixelated screen, the worn chair in the background a familiar but distant reminder of the life she once had.

She stares back at me. 'Are you talking to me?'

Clearly, today isn't a good day.

'How are you doing, Mum?'

'Who are you?'

'It's me, Mum - it's Melissa.'

A sadness enters her eyes. 'I once had a daughter called Melissa,' she tells me. 'Where is she? Who are you?'

'I *am* your daughter. Come on, Mum. I know I haven't seen you for a while but you *must* remember me.' A forced laugh escapes, masking the turmoil within. My heart silently weeps behind the screen. This is one occasion where I could do with her being lucid and loving. It's not just because of what's going on with Justin, it's also because of the life growing inside me. Mum was so involved when I was having Aisla and Ewan, and so excited. I'm just glad they can remember her before... this.

Well before we ever realised something was wrong, she would say, *if I end up not knowing who I am, who you are, or what day of the week it is, for goodness sake, put me out of my misery. I couldn't bear to do that to you all.*

But here we are. She's still in there somewhere and occasionally, she *does* still remember me, and even when it's only fleeting, I grasp it with every fibre of my being. If I only get a flicker of recognition from her while we're on this video call today, it will have been well worth it. I need her more than ever but it feels as though she's already gone.

'The kids send their love,' I say, continuing to fight back the tears. She doesn't need to see me crying - who knows what effect that would have on her.

'Who?'

Bloody hell. I choke back my tears and try to keep my voice steady. 'Aisla and Ewan. They're really missing you – we all are. I'd give anything to be able to hug you right now.' My voice cracks.

'I like hugs,' she says. 'I haven't had one for a while.'

'Me neither.' I wipe my face with my sleeve. A storm of conflicting emotions brews, knotting my stomach and sending shivers down my spine.

A sudden whoosh of cooler air beside my cheek startles me as an arm swoops around where I'm sitting.

Then a hand grabs at the laptop screen and slams it hard against the keyboard.

29

I push my chair back with a scrape and jump to my feet. For a moment I wonder if someone could have got inside the house. But, even as I swing around to look, I already know it's Justin.

'The minute my back's turned!' He rams his fist onto the top of the computer. First he's taken my phone from me and now this. I'm going to be lucky if it will power back on after what he's just done. I swipe it into the air and thrust it behind my back. I'll have to wait until he's out of the way to check that it still works. I can't risk him causing any further damage.

'I was only speaking to my mother.' I back away across the kitchen still holding the laptop against my back.

'What was it Melissa – were you hoping to get some money out of her? Money so you can leave me? I don't trust you one bit.'

'I just wanted to talk to her. What the hell is so wrong with that?'

'*What's wrong with that* is how you wait until my back's turned. Every. Single. Time.' He drives his finger into the table as he says each word.

'I only wanted to make sure she's alright. You ought to try checking on *your* mother.'

As soon as the words leave me, I'm only too aware of the dodgy ground I'm on. I've never met Judith Rose – she'd fallen out with Justin well before I came along and he wouldn't even invite her to our wedding. I've always been curious about her and now, more than ever, I'd love to hear her side of things.

'That woman's dead to me,' he replies, his jaw hardening. 'As you very well know.'

'Surely now more than ever, it would be a good time to get back in touch. With the virus and all that.'

'No chance.'

'Perhaps if you told her about the baby—'

'I don't want to talk about her.' He slams his palm onto the table. 'She completely sided with Lynette, for God's sake. What sort of mother does that?'

One who knows who you really are.

His attention is suddenly drawn to the piled-up shopping on the draining board. I take the chance to retreat even further from him. While he's staring at it all, I slip my laptop into the half-open drawer.

'You must still have some money stashed away *somewhere.*' He wags his finger in the direction of the sink. 'Since you've ordered this lot.'

Now I am baffled. 'I thought *you'd* ordered it.' Is he trying to mess with my head over the ordering of some groceries? I flinch as he comes towards me, relieved when he opens the fridge instead of coming at me.

'No. Like I already told you, I couldn't get anything delivered until the day after tomorrow.' The stink of beer fills the air as he pours it from the plastic bottle into a pint glass. The fresh air must have helped him to feel well enough to pour more of the stuff down his throat. If I'd been throwing up all night like he has, alcohol would be the last thing I'd want.

I cast my gaze over the shopping. All the basics have been delivered; bread, milk, eggs... 'I double-checked with the driver, Justin. He said the shopping was *definitely* meant for this address – he even checked my name when he came to the door.'

'So you *must* have ordered it.'

I stare at it all again. I can't have done. Unless this *baby brain* of mine is more addled than I've realised. No, I shake the thought away. I'm certain I would be able to recall placing a supermarket order!

'I didn't. Really, I didn't.'

'So someone must have ordered it *for* you.' He takes a long swig of his beer and then wipes the back of his hand across his lips. 'Who would do that?' His words are laced with suspicion.

'I've no idea. Perhaps it was Annie.'

The more I consider it, the more I think it can *only* be Annie. It's the sort of thing she'd do and she knows from our previous messages that I've got very little money, especially now.

As soon as I can get hold of my phone, I'll have to text or call to say thanks. I also need to apologise to Sue at the care home for so abruptly leaving the call with my mother. I hope she wasn't too confused or upset by it. And as for my kids - after our call was ended they *will* have been confused and upset. But there's nothing I could have done. And there's still nothing I can do. Not yet, anyway.

I begin filling the sink with water and washing up liquid. I might as well start wiping this lot over and putting it away.

'I'm going to have to sit down.' After a few minutes, Justin sinks to the chair I vacated. 'My stomach's still feeling off.'

I swing around to look at him. One hand's on his belly, the other is wrapped around his glass. 'Why don't you go to bed for a bit then?' What I mean to say is *why don't you get out of my way and leave me alone?*

Which is how he sees it too. 'Trying to get rid of me again, are you?'

'Of course not.' Here I go, pacifying him again. 'But if you're in pain—'

'A beer usually brings me round a bit when I'm feeling off.' He rubs at his belly. 'I'll be fine.'

Like I care. But then a thought occurs to me.

'A bad stomach isn't one of the symptoms of the virus, is it?'

'Is that all you're bloody bothered about?'

'No, but you have been out of the house a couple of times. Anyway, weren't you supposed to be getting a shower and changing your clothes?' I just want him out of the way so I can take a look at my computer.

'All *you're* bothered about is what I might pass to *you*. I never had you down as someone so selfish Melissa.'

'I'm not. I'm just concerned about you, that's all.'

He looks mildly placated by my words as he takes another gulp of his beer. Then the letter box rattles. We both look towards it and then at each other.

'Go and see what it is, will you?' I need to rest my stomach for a few minutes.'

He *must* be in pain. Usually, he'd be compelled to know about whatever it is. I head to the door to find a leaflet poking through. I tug a scarf from the coat hooks – at least then, I don't have to touch whatever it is directly before scanning it.

Oh my God. It's a leaflet for people who need to flee abuse during lockdown. Someone's posted a number for a bloody helpline through our door. If Justin sees this, he'll have a fit. I scrunch it into a ball in my palm. Thank God I got to it before he did.

I should probably be comforted by the fact that people around here are keeping an eye on me, but they have no idea of the additional trouble they're causing.

'What is it?' Justin leans against the kitchen doorway, still holding onto his midriff.

'What's *what*?' I tighten my fingers around the paper and hang the scarf over the bannister.

'Whatever was posted through just then?' He steps out of the doorway.

'Oh, it was nothing. Just some random leaflet.'

'So what have you got in your hand?' He nods towards it.

'Nothing.' Why didn't I just quickly stuff it in one of the coat pockets? This is me all over. *Act first, think later.* I need to be more focused and careful with what I'm doing around him. Every move I make at the moment has the potential to either make things more bearable for me, or to make things even more risky than they already are.

'Is it the leaflet?'

I nod. 'I'm just putting it in the bin. If I could just get past.'

He remains resolute in the centre of the hallway, the sunset casting a fleeting glow on his face. 'I want to see what it is before you do that.'

'It's just someone selling something.'

'During a global pandemic?' His face darkens. 'So why is your face bright red?'

I can feel it burning but I still touch it as if I'm doubting what he says. 'Is it?'

'Are you going to show me what it is or do I have to force it out of your hand?' He leans into the wall.

Right now, Justin looks as though he can barely stand up straight, let alone try to force something from me. Nevertheless, I'm not risking another confrontation. I just wish he'd leave me alone. Hopefully, he'll get as poorly as last night and clear off to bed.

'They're probably posting them through *everyone's* doors,' I say.

'I'm not letting you pass until you show me what it is.'

Torn between revealing the leaflet and keeping it hidden, I reluctantly straighten it and place it in his outstretched hand. 'I need to go and wash my hands.'

After a moment, he's behind me at the sink. 'Why are all these neighbours on my case, Melissa? What have you been telling them?' He paws at my shoulder as though trying to turn me around to face him.

'Nothing, just stop it, will you?' I twist my shoulder out of his reach. 'I need to get this shopping wiped down and put away if you don't mind.'

'And you can tell your *friend* we're not a charity case.' He lets go of my shoulder and returns to the chair. 'If her bloody husband would hurry and cough up what he owes me.'

'I thought you were happy with him leaving you the bottles of beer for now?' I gesture towards the porch.

'You still haven't answered my question.' He bends himself over the table. He seems to be having trouble even *sitting* straight.

'What question?'

'I want to know when you've been talking to the neighbours and what you've been saying.'

'When have I had the chance to talk to anyone? I haven't left the house for more than three weeks.' It feels like a lifetime and I still haven't found out whether the lockdown has been extended. The square is still as deserted as it has been so it must be carrying on.

'Before then, I mean. Why does everyone hate me so much? Don't you think my ex did enough damage to me without *you* jumping on the bandwagon?' He pulls a face. He really *is* in pain. Only a few months ago, I'd have been concerned about him, but now, I don't give a toss.

'It's a bloody leaflet, that's all. There's probably someone posting them through every single door on the square.'

'Go and see if they're still out there then.' He rocks forward and back, still clutching his stomach. 'I want to know what they think they're doing, pushing a leaflet like *that* through my door.'

'They're probably in another street by now. Honestly, just leave it alone, will you?'

He lets a pained noise out.

'You look awful Justin.' His face has an almost greyish tinge. 'You should go for a lie-down.'

'I'll finish my drink first.'

He takes another sip and grimaces. Then he screws the lid back on. 'Actually, you're right. On second thoughts, I'll just go. Bring me some water up, will you?'

I wait until all is quiet upstairs before sliding my laptop from the drawer. A wave of despair engulfs me as my fingers trace the massive dent he left on the laptop's lid. So many things have taken the brunt of his fist over the last three months. Walls, doors, the fridge and now *this*.

I hold my breath as I raise the screen. I can tell by the black zig-zag across it that it's damaged, even before I try to switch it on. And when I do, all I get is backlit blackness.

My chest tightens with resentment – I loathe him now more than I thought possible.

30

Fatigue tugs at my limbs, each step up the stairs a battle against a heavy pull. The dim light reveals Justin's figure, sprawled across the bed. Resisting the urge to chuck the glass of water I've fetched over him, I pull down the heavy blackout blind, shutting out the last traces of daylight. The room plunges into a dim twilight, shadows dancing across the curtains that I hastily draw over the blind. With a bit of luck, he'll stay right where he is until the morning. I certainly can't bear to be around him again tonight.

Kneeling beside his discarded jeans, I swipe my phone from the pocket, the silent act, a small rebellion against the chaos he's unleashed.

I've scrubbed my hands until they feel raw today but what if that isn't enough?

Justin's been to the chemist, as well as for a walk, and as he's said himself, I'm paranoid about the virus.

I've spoken to that policewoman, I got reasonably near to the delivery driver, I've handled the shopping, and then there was that leaflet that came through. I've put myself at more risk from the virus in one day than in all the days combined so far.

I scrub at myself some more in the shower, while wondering if I'm getting a sore throat. I'm more tired than normal too. *Extreme fatigue* is one of the symptoms of the virus. What if I've caught it? What will it do to me?

As I feared, the lockdown has been extended for another three weeks. It'll be May by then and I'll have been trapped with Justin for a whole six weeks. That's if we survive for that long.

The baby's doing somersaults inside me as I dry myself. *At least he or she is alright.* I'm supposed to be having my scan in a couple of weeks where I could find out if I'm having a girl or a boy, but I daren't go for it. The last place I want to be attending is a hospital. Until they get a vaccination or a cure, I daren't go *anywhere.*

I drag the joggers and t-shirt that I was wearing earlier back on. I haven't got many clothes that fit over my emerging bump now.

I pause outside the bedroom to check for Justin's snoring before returning downstairs. I won't be going anywhere near him tonight – no chance. I just hope he'll stay asleep, at least until I've called the kids, Annie, and the care home.

I step back as far as the charging cable will allow and perch myself on the edge of the lounge windowsill.

'Can I speak to Annie please?' I didn't expect Simon to answer her phone. He'd better not start a conversation with me. However, if he's got any idea that I know about his infidelity, he'll want to get me off the phone as quickly as possible. That said, he'll probably be punishing himself just as much as Justin's punishing him.

'She's doing a double shift.' He sounds as fed up as I am. Apart from delivering bottles of beer to his regulars, he's probably doing as little in terms of work as the rest of us. 'She called back home not so long ago to pick up her tablets, but went and left her phone behind.'

'Can you tell her I called please.' I nearly say *tell her thanks for the shopping* but it's got naff all to do with him. I can't bear to carry on any sort of a conversation – not after what he's done to my friend.

Dusk is falling over the square and like always, I welcome the opportunity to see into the homes that have their lights on but haven't yet drawn their curtains against the world. TVs flicker and people bob around in their lounges. I can't imagine any of the neighbours feeling as miserable and isolated as I do right now. Even Diane, who lives alone. From what I can gather she's got siblings and kids, whereas I feel as though I've got nobody at the moment.

My attention's averted to the young couple three doors along the square from Diane as they dart from their gate. One at a time, they dodge behind another neighbour's hedge and into the house, each clutching a bottle of some kind. I've noticed them countless times breaking the lockdown rules and going in there, giggling like naughty schoolchildren as they come and go.

What *she* won't know, however, is that I've also seen *him* sneaking countless times into Monica's house at all hours of the night. One of pregnancy's many 'gifts' is insomnia and this has given me more insight than I would have asked for into how some of the neighbours are carrying on around here. I'll never do anything about what I've seen: if I wasn't forced to shield myself from the outside world, perhaps I'd be breaking some of the rules too.

I glance into Monica's house. Her curtains are still open and she looks to be painting a wall. This is what many people seem to be doing with their unexpected time off – doing their homes up or sorting out their gardens. I'd love to be keeping busy like they are but I no longer have the money, nor the reason.

Movement from the upstairs flat next door to Monica catches my eye. *What's she doing?* I'm not sure. Hang on... The new neighbour appears to be gesturing at me but I can't make out what she's trying to say.

I shrug exaggeratedly as she repeats her actions. They're a mixture of holding her hand in the shape of a phone against her head and holding a suitcase against her window. Her gestures are as cryptic as a silent film. What's she trying to say? *Is she trying to tell me to leave here?*

Perhaps it's after the couple of visits the police have had to make. I throw my hands in the air as if to convey, *I haven't got a clue what you're trying to say.* Tomorrow, I'll try and hang around in our front garden again – perhaps then, I'll get a chance to actually speak with her.

31

MUM'S probably sleeping by now, however, it shouldn't be too late to call the children. My breathing quickens in anticipation of hearing their voices as I wait for the phone to be answered. Eventually being reunited with them is one of the only things that's keeping me going right now.

'Don't you think it's a bit late for this Melissa?' Rick sounds even more hostile than usual which must mean Cara is in range. I can always tell when she's not around as there's *slightly* more warmth in his voice. Slightly. But today, when I could use a little kindness more than ever, he sounds as cold as ice.

'Why – what are they doing? It's not *that* late.' I glance at the clock. On a *normal* night, they'd be getting to bed around this time, but nothing's normal for any of us at the moment.

'Ewan's just in the shower and Aisla's getting ready for bed.' I can almost see Rick's furrowed brow above his heavy-set eyebrows as he tries to get rid of me.

'Can't I just have ten minutes with them? Please, Rick.' Here I am, almost begging him to allow me to speak to my own children. This isn't right – how can he be so heartless? He knows me well enough to have a sense of how much I'm pining for them.

I try to catch what's being said amidst their muffled voices but the only thing I can be certain of is Cara spouting something about not wanting them to be upset before going to bed.

He clears his throat in readiness to speak again but I jump in first. 'With all respect, Rick,' I snap. 'I'm the children's mother, *not* Cara.'

'You don't know how upset the two of them were the other day,' he retorts. 'It took us ages to calm them down.'

He sounds weary too. It's been a while since he's been around the children twenty-four-seven for such an extended period. It wouldn't surprise me if before too long, he's beseeching me to take them back. Though *Cara* would probably try to stop him.

'You disappeared, *Melissa*.' He uses my name like he's chastising one of the kids. 'We tried and tried to call you back all day. What you did wasn't fair on them at all.'

'I'm sorry.' I can't exactly tell him how Justin cut me off and then confiscated my phone. It'll make me sound like a complete idiot. I don't want the kids getting a whiff of the trouble I'm in here, nor do I want Cara looking down her nose at me more than she already does. 'Really I am.'

'Look I'm not being funny, but can you call them back in the morning? Cara's right, you know. If they talk to you now, they'll never get to sleep.'

'I might not be able to.' Something inside me gives way at the realisation of how much under Justin's control I am.

'What do you mean, *I might not be able to.* Why *wouldn't* you?'

'Just tell them I love them, will you?'

'You can tell them yourself in the morning, if you don't mind.'

'Can you at least tell them I'm sorry about the other day?'

'I'm not saying *anything* to them – not if there's a chance you won't ring back when you say you will.'

In the background, Aisla's calling *Dad* which shatters my heart into a thousand pieces. It should be *me* she's calling for. They both feel so far away, yet I realise they're in the best place for now. I shudder to think of them embroiled in the situation I've managed to find myself in. At least, at their dad's, they're safely out of it all.

After I hit the 'end call' button, I continue staring over the square. Darkness has turned the vibrant green into a murky grey. The house is so quiet, I can literally hear the hiss of silence.

I open my Facebook app to see what's been going on in the new Facebook group while I've had no access to my phone or laptop. I've never posted anything into it but just to read the mundane messages helps me feel more connected to ordinary life.

> Does anyone have a pressure washer I can borrow? (I will wear brand-new rubber gloves while operating.)

> How's everyone doing in this crazy world?! Hope everyone is safe & well.

> If anyone is going to a supermarket at all over the weekend, please can you look out for some plain flour for me?

> Is anyone currently in isolation & struggling to get out for meals/food? I will have 2 spare roast beef dinners that I can leave on your doorstep in about 1 hr

I scroll through the endless posts, all in the same vein. And to think Justin was so set against me joining this group! What does he think will happen? I continue to scroll, paying extra attention to the days when the police have attended here. At least there's no mention of us.

I'd better get this phone back before he notices I've taken it. This might be what I'll have to do for now. Just keep sneaking it from his pocket, if that's where he continues to keep it, whenever I can. I can't risk him breaking it like he has with my computer.

I step into the hallway and stand at the bottom of the stairs for a few moments, comforted to feel the baby as he or she moves around me some more. It reminds me that I'm not completely alone. The soft snoring from the room above echoes through the quiet house, a rhythmic sound that both reassures and irritates me. When I go up, I'll slip the phone back where I got it from and he'll be none the wiser.

As I turn, I notice something else sticking out of the letterbox. I wrap my scarf around my hand again and tug it out. This time, it's a handwritten envelope, addressed to me. I pull out the note inside, which has been scribbled onto a scrap of paper.

> Hi stranger,
> I've been trying to text you - why aren't you answering me??
> I meant to say when we were messaging the other day that my offer still stands. (On both counts!) A place to stay and putting something in the food!!
> Hope you're OK - drop me a line when you get this.
> Annie xxx

She must have delivered it when I was in the shower. I can't believe she's put this through my door, knowing how things are for me. Justin could have so easily intercepted it. She clearly doesn't realise how unbearable things have become for me in here. At least before lockdown, I had some respite, as well as an escape plan.

Now I've got neither of those things.

I scrunch the note into a ball and bury it in the kitchen bin.

32

I sit up in bed and squint at the illuminated figures on my watch. 2:03 am. I don't know what's woken me this time, but something has. My heart is racing as though I've run for a bus and I'm sweating profusely – perhaps I've had a bad dream – thankfully one I seem unable to recall.

I navigate the room in darkness – the outline of the mirror where Aisla does her hair every morning, the TV she begged for until I eventually relented, the blown-up canvas of some pop star or other.

I turn over and nuzzle my nose into her pillow, only too aware that the scent of her in this room is beginning to fade. After more than three weeks, it's becoming more of an effort to conjure up in my mind what my children even look like and the thought brings the all-too-familiar sting of tears to my eyes.

I stiffen as there's a bang and then voices in the square. I bet it's that couple again - or the man sneaking in or out of Monica's house. Perhaps he's been caught in the act. His partner was bound to catch him sooner or later, carrying on right under her nose.

At this time of night, sound carries more than the owners of the voices seem to realise, especially if drink's been involved. I twist myself into a sitting position and swing my legs to the floor, swaying between indecision. Do I lean out of the window and ask them to keep it down, or do I just go and get a drink of water? Whatever I do, I just don't want Justin waking up. He's been sleeping since before seven and is likely to be in a foul mood after missing a whole evening of drinking and being able to keep an eye on *my* every move.

Slipping my arms into my dressing gown, I creep to the window and pull Aisla's curtain back slightly to peer around the edge of it.

The council have started switching some of the street lights off here at midnight, much to the disgust of many of the residents in the Facebook group, so it's difficult to see much apart from shadows and shapes. Even though the voices sound like they're raised, I can't seem to work out what's being said.

I hold my breath as I continue to watch and listen, pressing my burning forehead against the cooling sooth of the glass. I hope they don't notice me here, but there again, so what if they do – they shouldn't be carrying on like they are at two o'clock in the morning.

It's a woman and a man from what I can make out. However, the longer I listen, the more one of them *sounds* like it could be Justin. *Surely not.* As far as I know, he's fast asleep in the other room – I'm certain I'd have heard him moving around the house if he'd got up. And why would he be out there, carrying on with one of the neighbours anyway? Particularly *that* neighbour. The one he supposedly owes money to. My mind goes back to her holding a suitcase up at her window. *What the hell was she trying to tell me?*

My eyes grow more accustomed to the darkness until I can definitely say that it *is* him out there, prancing around, wearing only his dressing gown. His arms flail into the air as he says something to the woman and then kicks her gate. *What's going on?* I should march out there and demand to be told, but like Mum always used to say, *knowledge is power.* So for now, I'll just watch.

The neighbour returns to the doorway of the block of flats, also wearing a dressing gown.

'She has a right to know,' she declares, her words cutting through the night. Presumably, she's talking about me.

The realisation of what's going on hits me like a ton of bricks; Justin, in his dressing gown, is carrying on with the neighbour in full view and earshot of the entire square. I can't believe it.

I slump back onto the bed and bring my knees as close to my chest as the baby bump will allow. He's having an affair – he must be. I wonder how many more times he's sneaked out when I'm asleep?

A threat he's made several times swims into my thoughts. *Men who aren't getting it at home,* he has 'warned' me, *inevitably stray.*

No wonder that neighbour has been watching me so closely. I thought she was just bored with lockdown. Or plain weird.

Justin's creeping around downstairs now. Evidently, he doesn't want to wake me. The fridge door rattles. He must be getting the last bottle of beer.

I don't know how to feel – relieved because it looks like some other poor woman might take him off my hands – or angry. The more I analyse it, the more I think it's a combination of the two. He's treated me like shit since the turn of the year, yet he thinks he's got the right to add having an affair into the mix. All the while blackmailing his friend for doing the exact same thing.

One thing is for certain, I really can't continue to exist under the same roof as him for much longer – and certainly not under the nose of her across the way, if they *are* carrying on with each other. There's another three weeks, at least, to endure before the restrictions have a hope of being lifted. I'll go insane in that time.

Drawers open and close, and then the kitchen bin rattles. Suddenly, he's not making so much of an effort to keep his noise down.

Hearing his footsteps on the stairs, I slide down the bed, lay my head on the pillow and hold my breath, silently praying he'll just leave me alone.

But he's coming this way.

33

THE ROOM LIGHTS UP as Justin slams his palm against the switch.

'What the hell's this?' He storms over to the bed and thrusts something into my face.

'Ugh, geroff. What is it?' Whatever it is, it's wet around the edges. 'What time is it anyway?' If I act like I'm half asleep, he might go away and leave me alone.

'I want to know what this means.' He thrusts the soggy note under my nose, his eyes burning into mine. 'Annie's *offer* to put something in the food. Whose food? *Mine?*'

'Get away from me,' I hiss, forcefully pushing his clammy, intrusive hand aside, my skin crawling at his touch. 'It was just a joke, alright?' I shuffle off the end of the bed and stand up at the other side, watching as he swigs from his bottle. He's as attached to those beer bottles from Simon's pub as the baby will be to milk when it's born.

'I don't fucking believe you.' Justin's eyes narrow, a dangerous glint hinting at a deeper, unresolved issue beneath his paranoia. He holds the note aloft. 'Are *you* tampering with my meals, you *bitch*? Is that why my stomach's been so off it?' He shouts across the bed.

Any minute at all, he's going to go for me and my phone's back in his jeans pocket.

'Of course I haven't.' I tighten my dressing gown cord around myself. 'As if I'd do something like that.'

'Your nurse friend would though, wouldn't she? That's what it says here.'

'Unless you want the police back on the doorstep, I suggest you keep your voice down.'

'It'll be *you* and *her* they'll be carting off. God help you if I find out you've been messing with my food.'

'Well if you're worried, you could always cook for yourself. I'm not your bloody mother.'

'How *dare* you bring my mother up again? You do it on purpose, don't you?'

Maybe it wouldn't be such a bad thing if someone were to hear him carrying on and call the police. Right now, I can't envisage getting any peace from him for the rest of the night.

When the police come this time, I'm going to say, *take him – just take him.* I'll tell them how scared I am of him, which isn't a lie, and then they'll arrest him. I could even ask about him not being allowed back here – I might be able to get some sort of order against him.

Now I've seen him with that woman, I'm feeling braver about things. If I can get him out of here, it gives me more breathing space than the alternative.

'So when are you going to stay with her?' His nostrils flare as he continues to fix his steely gaze on me.

'Who?'

'Your nurse friend.'

'I'm not. I'm still here, aren't I?'

'Yeah, but we both know you'd be gone like a shot if it wasn't for the virus, don't we?'

I don't reply, which will probably anger him even further but so what? The more he yells, the more likely it is that someone will report him.

Mentioning the neighbour now might turn the tables, but fear and uncertainty hold me back. I need more before deciding my next move.

'You're enjoying all this, aren't you?' He sinks to the bed and takes a large gulp of beer while clutching at his stomach again. 'Seeing me suffer like this? I can't even stand up straight because of *you*.'

'*You're* the one who drinks like a fish.' I point at him. 'You can't stand up straight because of *you*.'

'I'm going to—' Clasping his hand over his mouth, he lurches back to his feet and races from the room.

I plug my ears, desperately trying to block out the gut-wrenching sounds of his retching from the adjacent room.

However, it's an excellent opportunity to get to my phone again. Maybe, by now, Simon will have said something to Annie about his new tenant. Now I know there's something more between her and Justin than an unpaid debt, I want to discover everything there is to know.

Simon said Annie was returning to work to do a night shift when I called earlier, so there's every chance she'll see if I message her.

Quick as a flash, I dart across the landing and into the pitch-black bedroom where Justin's clothes are still strewn. I exhale in relief as I put my hand on my phone. It's still where it was.

Then I dash past the bathroom where the sound of running water and Justin's pained groaning echoes from within. I wouldn't put it past him, however, to continue trying to get the rest of his beer down his throat.

I click Aisla's door closed behind me and burrow under her duvet, making sure my phone is still set to silent mode. I shoot a message to Annie, my fingers flying over the keys.

> Annie – it's me. I got your note. Are you awake? xx

I stare at the screen for a few moments, willing her to reply, even though it's now heading towards three in the morning. As my message blurs before my eyes, the bathroom door emits a low, ominous creak, a sound that crawls through the room like a ghostly whisper. Then the sound of shuffling across the landing carpet. I hold my breath as I wait to see which way he'll go. Back to bed or in here? I poke my head from the side of the duvet and stare at the strip of light beneath the door.

His shadow moves from side to side as though he's chasing indecision of whether to pursue his argument with me, or just take to his bed. Judging by the sound of him in there, he hopefully feels too ill to continue where he left off with me.

I let a long breath out as his bedroom door finally clicks shut, and nearly at the same time, my phone screen lights up with a text from Annie.

> I'm just in the staff room. I've been sent in to get my head down for a couple of hours. But I can't sleep. Are you OK? I'm glad you got my note. xx

> It sounds really tough for you – so never mind asking if I'm OK – are you OK? Justin saw it as well though. xx

I should probably get on with asking her what I need to ask her. After all, Justin could change his mind and still burst in here at any moment.

> I'm fine – it's what I was trained to do, after all. We're all feeling the strain but we'll get through it. And I'm so sorry about the note. That's why I put it in an envelope – so you'd get it and not him. xx

Our relationship doesn't work like that, unfortunately. Nothing I do is private. He's gone mad at your little 'joke' about his food. xx

Maybe he'll be a bit nicer to you now then. xx

Anyway, can I ask you a quick question then I'll let you try and get some sleep. xx

Sure. Fire away. xx

Has Simon said anything yet about the tenant in his old flat? Or did you ask him? xx

No, sorry – should I have done? xx

It's just, I think she and Justin might be seeing each other. I saw him sneaking out of her flat about half an hour ago. xx

Bloody hell. Do you really think he'd be carrying on right under your nose like that? xx

It certainly looks that way. xx

How do you feel? You're still planning on ending things, right? xx

Too right! I don't know how I feel, to be honest. A mixture of relieved, stupid, angry and baffled. She's been watching the house a hell of a lot and looked to be trying to tell me something earlier. I don't know if I should go over there and have it out with her. xx

I would. But just be careful. xx

I will. I'm going to sleep on it before I do anything. xx

Keep in touch. It worries me when you don't reply to my messages. xx

I'm sorry – but he keeps taking my phone. I've had to sneak it out of his pocket just to message you. xx

WHAT!!?? Bloody hell. The bastard. I can't believe it! xx

At least you know now. Just be careful about what you put through the door – I'm barely getting a moment's peace from him. He's watching nearly every move I make. xx

Heard and understood. I'll be really careful in future. But Melissa, you can't go on like this! xx

I don't think it will be for too much longer. Oh, and before I forget, thanks for the shopping you sent for me! xx

What shopping? xx

The other day – bread, milk and all that. Did you use your priority pass? xx

I'm sorry, I haven't had the chance to even shop for me and Simon, let alone you! xx

Well, that's strange. xx

I stare at the screen. If Annie didn't order it and Justin didn't, it *must* have been me. I'm sometimes guilty of doing things on autopilot but not remembering the placing of a grocery order is ridiculous.

Anyway, it doesn't matter. It must have been Justin. xx

I'm glad to hear he's doing something useful for once. You hang in there and hopefully, we'll get to see each other soon. xx

Night. xxx

34

I DON'T KNOW why I even bothered going to bed last night. I barely slept a wink.

I wrench the lounge curtains apart taking in the morning sun which casts a warm glow across the quiet square, revealing a tapestry of closed blinds in every window. The stillness of the square, with its neatly arranged houses and manicured lawns, paints a picture of suburban peace, broken only by *this* house and the neighbour's flat being in the midst of it.

I feel like marching over there, banging on the woman's door and demanding to know what's going on. I wonder if she has *any* idea of what she's dealing with. I know only too well how capable Justin is of portraying himself as a *nice guy*, but I've found out, to my cost, who he *really* is inside.

A large part of me is fuming that she deems it acceptable to carry on so blatantly with someone else's husband. She's no better than the neighbour I've observed sneaking in and out of Monica's house since we locked down. We women should stick together and support one another – not run off with each other's husbands.

For all she knows, she could be breaking up a marriage that's worth saving – she obviously doesn't have a clue of my plans to leave. She must have moved onto this square with an agenda – to get closer to Justin. I sensed something between them on that first day of lockdown but was too focused on my own misery to give it enough attention. And I'm bewildered at how he's got the brass neck to blackmail Simon for something he's guilty of doing himself.

I can clearly pinpoint when the wheels came off in our marriage. Christmas Eve – when I believed the catalyst to be Cameron telling him where to go. I've never met Justin's son but his hatred for his father was evident from what I could hear of his voice echoing across the room. He was spitting venom about how cruelly Justin had treated his mother. Eventually, Justin cut him off and threw his phone onto the sofa.

That was the start of his endless Christmas drinking. My kids couldn't go anywhere near him without being bellowed at and he was sick all over the hallway. Just the three of us ate our Christmas Dinner while he went back to The Old Crown for a lock-in Simon had organised while Annie was working. At least that's where he *said* he was going.

Only now, can I see that he'd already checked out of our marriage. He'd found someone else – someone with whom he'd been conducting a relationship in the middle of the night. There's been many a night when I've woken and he hasn't been beside me. He's blamed insomnia, he's told me he's been watching films, but now I know the truth. He's probably been sneaking to *her* door.

A glimpse of my haggard reflection catches my eye as I pass the mirror. The stark contrast of my almost black roots against my straggly blonde hair and the dark circles under my eyes tell of the sleepless weeks I've endured. It's a combination of so many things. The virus, Justin, missing my kids, my hormones, my mum. I don't think I've ever felt this miserable in my life.

Pregnancy should be a joyful time, but for me, it's turned into the darkest and most lonely period I've ever endured. I can't turn to

Mum any more, Annie's too overwhelmed with work and I've barely heard from my workmates. Not directly anyway – only in the WhatsApp group.

I tug my phone from my dressing gown pocket – partly for the familiarity of seeing what they're all up to – and also to see if anyone's posted about when we can expect to get any money from the hotel.

> Getting bored with all this now – how's everyone else doing?

> Busy decorating. My house is looking like a palace.

> Kids are doing my head in – I take my hat off to those teachers, that's all I can say.

> Wall-to-wall sunshine. Plenty of wine and at home with the husband. What's not to love?

> Apparently, we can expect a month's pay on the 20th folks. Well, 80% of what we'd normally get.

> It's better than a kick in the teeth.

> About time.

Eighty per cent of my wage will give me nearly what I'll need for the letting agent. *The twentieth.* That's only three days away. There's still well over a fortnight to go until there's any chance of the restrictions being lifted. So as soon as the money comes into my account, I'm transferring it to Annie for safekeeping. I can't risk Justin getting his hands on it again.

That's if he's still here on the twentieth. With everything that's going on, *anything* could happen. Particularly if I confront him with what I saw last night.

I'd better text Annie so she knows what the money is when it hits her account. I'd better be quick since I've only got 2% of the battery left on my phone. He took my charger up with him last night so there's no way I can get it at the moment.

> It's only me. I'm getting paid on the 20th. Just checking that it's OK if I transfer the money to you so Justin can't get his hands on it??? xx

By the time I've made a cup of tea and toast, she hasn't answered. So I text again. I'm down to 1% now.

> I've already got your details somewhere from when we went to that spa day in December, so don't worry about sending them to me. xx

December. When life felt normal. Before we had any idea all this was in store.

It might be a good idea to get Annie's bank details set up *now* before my battery completely dies, so she's a payee on my account already. That way, on the 20th, I can quickly log in the moment the money hits my account and transfer it out to her without any messing.

I cast my gaze around our sunny lounge, at our wedding photo on the sideboard and the fleecy rug I brought from our last house. I might have loved this place once, but now, I can't wait to get out of here.

On my way to the kitchen, I hear what sounds like a thud on the porch. I tiptoe to the door and peer through the spy hole. *It's the woman from the flat.* It's all I can do not to wrench the door open and let rip at her. However, nothing's worth waking Justin for before he's ready to get up.

I watch as she lingers for a few moments, wondering if she can somehow sense me at the other side of this door.

As she walks away, I see she's left some milk and bread next to

Justin's bottles of beer. Clearly, her intentions aren't what I thought they were...

I creep to the kitchen and close the door behind me. If memory serves me correctly, I wrote Annie's account details on the edge of a gas bill. I should have saved them to my account but I didn't expect to be transferring any more money to her.

I rifle through the drawer where Justin stuffs things like bills and letters. He was here long before me so his name's on all the household accounts – all I've ever done is transfer him my half for it all each month since I moved in. I know exactly what I'm looking for – I can picture the numbers scribbled in a red pencil I'd grabbed from Aisla's pencil case.

I can't imagine Justin throwing the statement away – he rarely does. Mostly, he just shoves everything in the drawer he's dubbed *his filing system* for the day that never comes. I've always been jokingly told to keep out of 'his drawer' and have often been tempted to have a rifle through. Now's my big chance.

Several flashes of red print catch my eye as I leaf through the envelopes and letters but there's no sign of the statement I'm looking for.

As I return to the top of the pile to have another go, an envelope from the Yorkshire Building Society catches my eye. It would be interesting to see how much he still owes on the house. I tug it from the drawer and slide the letter out.

35

THERE, in bold red type is a demand for £9439. Mortgage arrears that *are to be cleared immediately*. If the threat in the letter had been carried out, the 'matter' should have been passed to the court by now. Even if everything that's happened between us had *never* happened, we'd still be facing being out on our ear in the not-too-distant future.

Mortgage holders have been granted a reprieve since lockdown started but as soon as the restrictions are lifted, the Yorkshire Building Society will, no doubt, be repossessing this house, especially with *that* level of arrears. All the money I've paid him to live here with the children – *what the hell has he done with it?*

Joining that letter is another one, further evidence of Justin's debt – Council Tax arrears, a disconnection threat, letters from a debt collection agency and then...

An A4-sized brown envelope franked with Yorkshire County Court is the second to last envelope in the drawer. I tug it from beneath everything else and slip the papers out. It's the decree nisi from his and Lynette's divorce. I've already seen his decree absolute which he had to produce to get married to me.

I cast my mind back to that day. March 2nd last year. It was only a small registry office wedding but everyone I cared about was there. Annie, Simon, some other friends from the pub and friends from work. At least, I thought they were friends. Since the start of lockdown, everyone seems to have disappeared. Aisla and Ewan were my flower girl and page boy and one of the carers brought Mum. When Justin and I stood facing each other while holding hands in front of the registrar, all I saw was happiness and stability ahead of us. How I misjudged it all.

My breath feels constricted and the grip around my chest is almost vice-like. I need my inhaler. I open the drawer next to the one I'm rifling through for my spare but there's no sign. I'm almost certain I returned it. I don't remember using it up, but my head has been all over the place lately. I'll get my other one from upstairs as soon as he gets up. In the meantime, I don't want to disturb him unless I have to.

I turn back to the first drawer, trying to steady my breathing. If I remain focused on something else, it should improve.

Beneath the decree nisi are the pages of their divorce petition. *Interesting.*

He's told me yet another lie. Justin's story was that *he'd* divorced Lynnette for unreasonable behaviour – he claimed she was belittling him, seeing other men, and banking secret accounts of money while frivolously spending *his.*

But most importantly, she was poisoning Cameron, their son against him. She hadn't contested the divorce, he said – which was further evidence of her guilt.

But according to what I'm reading here, it was the other way around. She divorced *him* for unreasonable behaviour. I flick to the page where Lynette's 'particulars' have been listed, my jaw dropping a little more with every item I read.

The Respondent has been physically abusive towards the Petitioner, causing bruising and injury to her arm, which has left her worried for her safety.

The Respondent has made repeated threats towards their son when he has tried to intervene and protect his mother.

The Respondent is regularly verbally abusive towards the Petitioner and their son, which they find belittling and distressing. The Respondent has continued with this abuse, despite being told how it makes the Petitioner and their son feel.

The Respondent has incurred large debts which have threatened the security of the family home. He refuses to take any action to address these debts.

The Respondent has taken out financial agreements in the Petitioner's name without her knowledge or consent.

The Respondent regularly consumes excessive amounts of alcohol which the Petitioner finds unacceptable.

The Respondent is only willing to hold down gainful employment for brief durations, causing all of the financial responsibility to be placed onto the Petitioner.

No wonder he guarded this drawer like a fortress – though part of me can't understand why he's even kept hold of a document like this.

He wouldn't have been able to evade her claims either. Everything she's alleged is backed up with references to police visits, photographs and witness statements.

He led me to believe the breakup was all Lynette's fault. That *she'd* been the cruel and abusive party, turning their son and everyone else against him, even his mother. But here it is, in black and white, with evidence to back it up. And my own divorce petition against him will read in a similar way.

Lastly, right at the bottom of the drawer is another envelope of a similar thickness to the divorce paperwork. The first page is what seems to be a copy of a remortgage agreement which has been signed by him and Lynette. It's stamped with an *evidence* stamp. Then there's a credit card agreement signed by Lynette, a loan agreement, and a car finance application – they've all been signed by Lynette and similarly stamped as evidence. Bloody hell –he's been forging her signature to obtain his funding.

Next is a court summons. I check the date on my watch. He would have been on trial at Yorkshire Crown Court, charged with fraud *last week,* had it not been for the lockdown. It's dated 19th December. There's another reason for the sudden change in his behaviour at Christmas. It also goes some way towards explaining why he's barely gone to work since.

Lastly, there's a transcript of what looks like a police interview and a couple of solicitor letters. They mainly date back to November. I'm baffled that he's managed to keep all this a secret from me. I settle down at the kitchen table to read through it all.

'What the *hell* are you doing?' Justin's voice slices through the air.

My head jerks to where he looms in the doorway, looking from me to the drawer I've left open.

Shit.

36

'I SAID – WHAT ARE YOU DOING?'

'I, erm, I was just looking for my spare inhaler. I didn't want to come upstairs and disturb you.'

'Amongst my private papers? You know that's *my* drawer.' Justin's face is grey and drawn. He still looks dreadful but clearly anger's taken over how ill he's feeling.

For a moment we just stare at each other. I don't know what to do or what to say for the best. It's not just that – I'm also in shock with everything I've just discovered in that drawer.

That his ex-wife was treated just like I've been, that this house is about to be repossessed. And that he could be facing prison for fraud. Although knowing Justin, he'll manage to lie his way out of it all. I guess Lynette would have to *prove* she didn't sign any of those agreements and it could just come down to her word against his.

I'm certain that Justin, with his many personas, will simply choose his mask of superficial charm when it's court day and say all the right things to steer the jury towards him, especially the female jurors.

A realisation steals over me that I probably need to check *my own* credit reports. Who knows what he might have taken out in *my* name?

The thought hits me like a cold shower. Maybe I'm on some blacklist, the reason why the rented house slipped through my fingers three weeks ago. The walls here are really closing in on me, with secrets lurking in every corner. The letting agent had previously assured me the place was mine but he might have been just fobbing me off when he said the other couple weren't moving out after all.

Justin finally breaks the deadlock between us. 'You had no right reading things that don't concern you,' he blurts. '*No right at all.*' He steps towards me and plucks the envelope from my hand, before swiping at the papers on the table.

'Why haven't you told me about all this?' My voice is breathless as I gesture to what *he's* now holding. I need to sit down. I don't know what's going to happen here but this feels like it isn't going to end well at all.

'*You.*' He points at me, hatred etched across his unshaven face. 'You've turned out to be every bit as nasty and vindictive as *she* is.'

'From what I've read in there...' I point at the open drawer. 'Blame is only on *your* side, not Lynette's.'

'So you're using her name now – you don't normally do that.' His voice rises a notch. 'What is it Melissa – have you *completely* turned on me? Have you gone onto *her* side, like my son and my mother?'

'You've told me a complete pack of lies.' I rest my hands on my belly. It's as though I'm reminding him of our baby's existence, in case he has any inclination to get as violent with me, as it appears he was with Lynette.

'Women have always been the downfall of my life,' he snarls as he rams the envelopes back where I got them from. '*Everything* that's *ever* gone wrong for me in life has a woman at the root of it.' He slams the drawer so hard, it makes me jump.

I freeze as the letterbox rattles. *Now what?* I pray it's only the post and not a well-meaning neighbour posting something else in a misguided attempt to help me.

I start to get back up but Justin beats me to it and is first towards the front door. He grabs at the letters which have been posted, but beneath them is a scrap of paper. He glances at it, before clenching it within his fist.

It's a fist he'd probably like to use on me given half a chance. Being pregnant is probably my saving grace here. Though if Justin *was* going to hit me, surely he'd have done it before today?

'Is that note for me?'

'No – it bloody isn't. Just leave me alone will you?' He turns back towards the door and I take the opportunity to make for the stairs.

'Get back here. We haven't finished with this yet?'

I pause in my tracks. 'You've just told me to leave you alone.'

'You know exactly what you're doing, don't you? You've turned out just like *she* did.'

He opens the front door, making me wonder if he's going to go after whoever put the note through. Instead, he reaches down and collects a two-litre bottle of beer in each of his hands, leaving the milk and bread that was left out there.

Gosh, why can't I just have a normal life? Why can't I be painting a fence, baking banana bread or homeschooling my kids like everyone else is?

'I need a beer,' he mutters as he heads back towards the kitchen.

'Of course you do,' I also mutter, keeping my voice low so he can't hear me as he clatters about to find a glass in the dishwasher.

'And we still need to talk, so get in here.'

I'll hang on until he's sitting at the table with his beer. Then I'll pretend I need the loo, get my phone on charge and take my inhaler.

'I take it your plans will be back on to leave me?' He surveys me through narrowed eyes as he brushes beer froth from his top lip and sits in his usual spot at the kitchen table.

'I can't go *anywhere* at the moment, can I?' I sigh as I loiter in the doorway. Now he's got his beer, he seems to have calmed down.

'No, but you would if you could, wouldn't you?' His voice hardens as he drives his finger into the table. 'Like. A. Shot.'

I'm sick of the way he looks at me. I'm even sicker of the way he speaks to me. So I'm going to take him down a peg or two.

'I saw you last night – over there.' My voice remains low as I nod towards the block of flats. 'So, instead of blaming me, or Lynette for everything that's ever gone wrong in your life, you should look at your own behaviour. What were you doing?'

He gulps back nearly half the glass of his beer in one go, the condensation leaving a ring of moisture on the table. 'What the hell are you talking about?'

'The woman who's just moved in over there. What's *really* going on?'

My eyes don't leave his as I wait for his reaction.

37

'I DON'T KNOW what you're talking about.'

So he's playing dumb. I thought he might. 'I saw you both in the middle of the night – carrying on in full view of the entire square. Don't try telling me it's over some *owed money* because I don't believe you.'

Sarcasm will probably not do me any favours, but right now, I'm at my wit's end and don't know what to do for the best. I just know that I can't go on like this. I've survived over three weeks in this way and don't think I can go on a moment longer. As time passes, Justin's becoming increasingly unhinged and I'm feeling less and less safe being alone in the house with him.

I should allow what's going on today to escalate to an explosive row. Diane, Monica or one of the other immediate neighbours will hear us. My mind races through desperate scenarios. A call to the police, a change of locks – anything to break free from this suffocating situation. Then I can ensure he's taken away this time, and forced to stay somewhere else if and when he's released. If I tell the police how scared I am of him, they'll help me – that's what they said.

Or maybe there's another way through all this – something

much more final. The baby's jolting around inside me, his or her movements like a silent plea, a reminder that I'm not alone in this turmoil, and perhaps also reminding me that I have to remain vigilant and extra cautious in how I deal with him.

'I heard noises.' He stares into his glass. 'I thought someone was breaking in so I went out to stop them.'

So he's going down that line with me.

'That's the lamest thing I ever heard.' I could almost laugh at his explanation if the situation wasn't so dreadful between us. 'So if that's the case, what were the two of you arguing about? Surely she'd have been grateful if you were investigating some so-called *noises*.'

'She thought it was *me* trying to get in.' He rakes his fingers through his hair. I've never seen it so greasy and in need of a wash. 'She caught me peering through the windows into the main entrance.' He looks up at me as though imploring me to believe him. 'Then she wouldn't believe I was only there because I was trying to help.'

'Why can't you just tell me the truth, Justin?'

'Because it is the fucking truth!' He leaps from his chair then his features contort as his hand clenches against his stomach.

One thing is for certain – I've never heard him yell so loudly. He's crimson in the face and looks to be almost frothing at the mouth. Yet he bends forward to take another gulp of his beer. I can smell the hops from here – it smells vile. I don't know how he can drink the stuff.

I back away from him, moving myself to the opposite side of the kitchen. Judging by his demeanour, he's likely to fly at me, baby or not any moment now. His current mood is worse than anything I've ever seen.

I press my back against the kitchen wall, the cool surface providing a momentary respite as I struggle for breath. I've become even wheezier since he came downstairs and caught me in that drawer. I need to get past him and get to my inhaler. I've left it for long enough.

The baby's fluttering away inside me, probably somersaulting with the stress that's no doubt passing from me to him or her. I have to sort this out. I've affected my two older children enough with this second marriage I lurched into, without inflicting it all on a third child.

'Aaargh.' Suddenly, he's bent forward and clutching the edge of the worktop. 'I don't know what's bloody wrong with me.'

'Is it your stomach again?'

'What would you care?' He reaches for his glass and takes another gulp. I've never seen anything like it. Someone who's so unwell and in pain yet continues to throw alcohol down their neck.

In the past, he's often joked about needing to drink the next morning *for medicinal purposes* – to numb his hangovers. But this behaviour's in another league altogether.

There is, however, another possibility... That he's putting on this little charade of being in agony to detract from himself – from what I saw last night and what I've found in the drawer this morning. He might be hoping that I'll let up on him if he's ill.

'Maybe you should sit down.'

He staggers to the table and lands on a chair. 'I've never felt this ill. Maybe I've caught the virus or this beer has all been *off*.' He stares back at the glass he left on the counter. 'Maybe that's why Simon's been so keen to get rid of it,' he continues. 'Or... *the bastard*. I reckon he's been lacing it with something – thinking that if he finishes me off, he won't have to pay up.' He staggers back to his feet and back over to the bottle he left on the counter.

He picks it up and then sniffs at it. Then he drops his glass to the floor where it smashes at his feet. He lurches to the sink, which he then leans over, retching into it.

As I turn away in disgust, I notice the crumpled note which he must have dropped. While he's preoccupied throwing up the beer he's drunk this morning back up his throat, I rush to pick it up.

Melissa. You need to get out of there. Ring this number and I'll tell you everything. Lynette

Then she's written her number.

Justin looks at me with red-ringed eyes and drool dripping from his mouth. I need to get some charge on my phone to find out what she's got to say. I don't know what she could be planning to tell me that I haven't found out already. And why she's suddenly contacting me *now?*

'You and her are NOT speaking to each other,' he bellows as his eyes fall on the note in my hand. 'Do you think I'm going to let you pair of witches pull a number on me.' He staggers towards me. In the state he's in, I doubt he'd be able to do much damage but I'm not taking any chances.

I rush towards the steps. I'm going to grab my charging lead and my inhaler, then get myself out of the house. I'm finding it more difficult to get my breaths in so I need to get to my inhaler fast.

He lands on the floor and lunges at my legs just as I reach the bottom step, toppling me forward onto the stairs.

'Get away from me.' Holding onto the bannister, I kick out at him to push him back. Surprisingly, he summons more strength than I credited him with, his movements betraying an unpredictable resilience. He's soon back on his feet, shoving me out of the way so he can get up the stairs ahead of me.

He won't know that I've retrieved my phone from his pocket so that's what he must be going for. I rush after him and manage to grab a fistful of the back of his dressing gown but he spins around and wrenches it out of my grasp.

'Let me past. Please Justin, I need to get to my inhaler.' After our scuffle at the bottom of the stairs, my breathing has suddenly become sharp and painful. I know the signs. If I don't get the

Ventolin into me within the next few minutes, I'm going to have a full-blown asthma attack. Surely he won't try to prevent me from getting to my inhaler? If I can just get into that bedroom before him, I can grab my charger while I'm at it too. I'm going to call the police – things have gone too far this time.

'Aaargh.' He gets to the closed bedroom door before me and doubles up in pain against it. 'You've probably done this to me, you bitch, you must have done.' He slides down to the floor. 'It's *you*. You're trying to do me in, aren't you?'

'Just let me get in there,' I gasp. It's getting more difficult to speak. I should have taken it the minute I began wheezing. Mum always used to go mad at me for pushing my luck with my asthma. 'You don't realise what a life-threatening condition it can be,' she would say.

He's got sick all down his dressing gown and something awful-looking around his mouth. I can hardly bear to look at him but he needs an eye keeping on him right now. He might be ill but he's still unpredictable.

Suddenly, he finds the strength to rise back up against the door to his full height again. I try to go around him but he pushes me back into the landing wall. My back connects squarely with it and for a moment, I'm winded and even more unable to get my breath in than before.

Tendrils of despair wrap around me as he lurches into the bedroom and wrenches open the drawer of my dressing table where I keep my inhaler.

'No!' The word should be a shriek but comes out like more of a whisper.

As I haul myself back onto my feet, he's already pressing it over and over again. He's bloody emptying it and I don't know where my spare is!

I tug my phone from my pocket. As I'd feared, the battery has died.

I lurch towards where my charging cable is usually plugged in but he gets there first as well.

Then I spot *his* phone, plugged in at his side of the bed and begin edging myself around towards it.

Seeing what I'm doing, he drops my inhaler to the ground before stamping on it.

I pummel at his screen. If I can just get an emergency call to connect before he reaches me, the police will trace the call and get here.

'Good luck with that one,' he says from the doorway.

His phone is also dead.

38

As I GRAPPLE around the room for my charging cable, Justin's returned to the top of the stairs. I can't find it. *I need to get out into the square for help.*

I stagger after Justin.

'No!'

The kitchen echoes with the repeated hiss of an inhaler.

My chest constricts, and I gasp for air, clutching at my ribs. I lurch along the hallway and lean into the kitchen doorframe.

Justin's sprawled on the floor against the cupboard, his dressing gown flapping out all around him while he presses the button on my inhaler for all he's worth. *I did have a spare.* Either I put it in a different place or *he's* moved it.

'Please – stop!'

After several seconds, he aims it at my head and it's obvious by the hollow thud it makes as it lands at my feet, that he's emptied it, like he did with the other one.

'What – are – you – trying – to – do?' The journey up and down the stairs and wrestling with him on the landing has made everything much worse. I'm having to take a breath between each word. I need to get to a hospital – fast.

I stumble to the back door. It's locked. 'Where – are – the – keys? I rummage around in the drawer they're normally kept in.

'Two can play your game Melissa. If I'm going down, you're coming with me.' He strikes out from where he's slumped and grabs hold of my wrist.

'Get – off – me.' I try to wrench my arm free. I have to get help and I have to get it quickly.

'You're going nowhere.'

His pain must be weakening him because I manage to break free of his grip and push past him. I've now got a chance to get out of the *front* door.

But it's also locked.

My eyes flit from the table to the windowsill. He's emptied both my inhalers. He's cut off my access to a phone and now he's hidden the keys to both doors. He wants to kill me, that much I know. *I've got to get away from him.*

With my back against the wall, I bend forwards, gasping as I try to get some breath in. The panic is making it ten times worse. I try to slow it down, remembering Mum's words when I was young. *That's it Melissa. Breathe in – slowly, fill your tummy up with air. Now slowly out. Calm and slow. Count to three. In – and – out. It's all going to be alright.*

Summoning my last reserves of strength, I stand tall, pounding my fists against the door. Each hit echoes the desperation pulsating through me. 'Help.' My voice is a rasp. I can only pray that someone's passing by and they hear me banging.

Justin suddenly grabs me from behind, his fingers boring into my shoulders.

'Let – me – get – help.' With one hand, I reach to prise his fingers from my opposite arm but his grip is vice-like and he isn't letting go. 'Get – off – me.' I kick backwards and he groans as my foot connects with his shin.

Miraculously, he lets me go.

I make it into the lounge and my fingers fumble for a lifeline as I tug at the heavy curtain.

'Help – me – someone!' I beat the palm of my hand against the glass. 'Help!' No one's going to hear me. I look up to where that woman has spent three weeks gawping into our house – now she's nowhere to be seen. I'm done for. Unless I let someone know what's going on in here, I'm well and truly done for.

Meanwhile, Justin's on his hands and knees behind me, grabbing at my legs again, rugby tackle style, in the same way he did when we were at the bottom of the stairs.

He forces me to the floor and I try to kick out at him, but my limbs feel like lead, drained of energy. My airway feels like it's just about closed. I try to gulp some air in. *Breathe in – breathe out.* It's Mum again. *That's it. Try and slow it down. Calm down – you're going to be alright.*

He's clambering on top of me – he's pinning my arms above my head. His crushing weight presses my hips into the floor and it feels as though it's squeezing the last of any oxygen from me.

'No.' My word is barely audible.

The look in his eyes is wild. Any minute now his hands are going to move to my neck and then it's all over.

Suddenly he cries out and his weight releases from my chest. Then he rolls away from me, bringing his knees to his chest and grabbing at the front of his head. 'Aargh, my head,' he yells, rolling from side to side. 'It's killing me. What have you done to me? I can't see anything.'

'I – need – help – the – baby.' My head rolls to one side. My face is now staring into his.

My lips are probably as blue as his are. We're not going to make it out of here. Any of us. My baby – I've got to save my baby. If I just lie here for a moment and try to find some calm, my breath might come back. I can survive this. I know I can. I've got to. My kids. They need me.

'The room's spinning.' Justin closes his eyes. 'You did this to me. It's all your fault.'

I'm not going to make it. Mum was right about my asthma – it's about to claim my life. I close my eyes. I'm almost out of fight. The faces of my children flash before me, fleeting images in the dwindling light of consciousness.

Someone's hammering at the window. *Thank God.* I want to raise my arm – to let whoever it is know I'm still alive, but when I try, I'm unable to move. I force my eyes back open and try to focus. Is someone looking through the gap I've left between the curtains? I'm almost certain it's the woman from the flat.

I don't think I've ever had an asthma attack this serious. And I always had my mother taking care of me while help was on its way. The knowledge it was coming was calming in itself. As my eyes fall closed, a vision of her with her curled hair and pink lipstick swims into my mind. I hear her voice. 'Keep calm Melissa. Help's on its way.'

In the hazy dance between reality and nothingness, the letterbox rattles, a discordant sound in my fading awareness. A voice echoes amidst the rasps of what are possibly my dying breaths.

But it's not my mother's voice.

'Melissa, it's Lynette out here – Lynette Rose. Justin's ex-wife.'

Lynette? *The Lynette?*

I must be hallucinating. After all, why would *she* be here? I attempt to move again but can't seem to muster anything. I haven't even got the strength to open my eyes.

'I've seen you through the window Melissa. There's an ambulance on its way. And the police. Just hang in there for me.'

For me?

'I only ever wanted to help, you know – to keep an eye on you. I know Justin better than anyone. We all wanted to help but haven't been able to get anywhere near you. Look – if you can hear me, I'm sorry. I truly am. My best wasn't anywhere near good enough.'

The letterbox snaps shut. My chest feels like it's going to explode with the exertion of trying to get another breath in. Any one of these could be my last.

There's no way they're going to get to me in time.

LYNETTE

39

'Come on, come on, come on.' I dart up and down the path then back again. The sirens are conspicuously absent, leaving a void that amplifies the silence.

I press my face up to the window once again – to see if there's been any change. From what I can see through the gap in the curtains, the two of them are lying fairly close to one another on the floor. I've no idea what's happened in there for them *both* to end up that way but neither of them are moving. They both appear to be unconscious but I bang on the window again – just in case.

'Melissa,' I shout. 'Melissa, if you can hear me, move your arm.'

I don't even know why I've asked that. Due to the curtains, the room is in semi-darkness. It was virtually impossible to determine any sign of life when I was on the phone with the emergency services. Or death.

'What are *you* doing?' Diane steps from her car and reaches for the shopping bags on her passenger seat. She's been my lifeline over the years and at this moment, she's a more welcome sight than ever.

'Bloody hell. I'm so glad to see you.'

'What on earth are you looking at?' Frowning, she dumps the bags behind her gate and hurries over to me, stopping short of the two-metre distance we're all so accustomed to.

'Something's happened.' I can't hold back the tears anymore. 'Look.' I gesture to the window.

She tucks her greying hair behind one ear and presses her face up to the glass. 'Oh my goodness. Is she—? Are they—?'

'I don't know – I can't get in there.' I swipe the back of my hand over my eyes. My crying isn't going to achieve anything. 'All the doors and windows are locked. We knew it might end like this, didn't we?'

'We'll just have to break in.'

Diane's demure frame is about the same as mine. Throwing our weight against anything is hardly likely to cause much of an impact. We're both wearing knee-length shorts and sleeveless tops so will probably shred our limbs to smithereens if we start trying to smash our way through the windows. 'You know as well as I do that these houses are like Fort Knox once they're closed up,' I remind her.

'I'll grab a hammer then, shall I?' Before she's even finished speaking, she's already heading in the direction of her house.

I flit back around to the front door and bend to the letterbox again. 'Melissa, can you hear me?' I call. 'If you can, try and make a sound, so I know you're OK.'

I pause. Nothing.

'Diane's here now too,' I continue. 'We're going to try and get into you.'

'Don't you think you should leave it to the police?' The neighbour directly facing us folds her arms as she watches from behind her gate. No doubt she'll have seen and heard as much as I have over the last three weeks. It's been awful, being so near and yet so far – being powerless to intervene.

'No, I do not. If we get in there now, she might have a chance.'

Diane hurtles back towards me with a hammer in her hand.

'Give it to me,' I hold my hand out. Somehow it feels better that it's *me* smashing a window into the house I used to own.

'Smash the glass in the door,' Diane urges. 'They might have left the key in.'

'I doubt it,' I reply. 'But I'll try.'

The frosted window gives on the fourth attempt and I smash the remaining shards of glass around the edge of the frame to give me easier access when reaching round to the lock. As I suspected, there's no key. There's every chance Justin might have moved the keys to prevent Melissa from leaving. He used to do that with me. Nor is the window big enough for me to climb through.

'Melissa, we're nearly in,' I shout into the hallway. 'Can you hear me?'

All I can hear is my own voice echoing back from the hallway I used to leave and enter every day. I wasn't prepared for its familiarity. But I can't think about that now.

'I'm going to have to try the lounge window,' I tell Diane.

'What if it's *too late*?' She closes her eyes for a moment. 'Oh, the poor dear girl. And that baby. It would have been Cameron's half-brother or sister, wouldn't it?'

'Don't say *would have been*. That implies—'

'I know. I'm sorry.' She looks from me back towards the window.

'What's going on?' Another neighbour's curious voice interrupts from behind me.

'Just stand back, will you?'

It takes two swings of the hammer to shatter the glass in the bottom section of the window. But it's double-glazed. If I can just manage to smash my way right through it, I'll be able to climb through.

'Be careful Lynette – you're bleeding.'

'I don't care. We've just got to get into her.'

I continue slamming the hammer against the window, finally managing to break right through the first pane, if I can just knock some of this glass out of the way, I can get through the second pane.

'Did you tell them how serious it is?' Diane asks. 'That one or both of them could be dead?'

'Dead?' Someone gasps from behind me. 'Oh my God.'

'Oh my goodness, finally.'

Two police cars screech around the corner. A third siren is still echoing around this usually peaceful village. Hopefully, it's an ambulance.

As half a dozen masked officers leap from their vehicles and usher us out of the way, more neighbours begin to appear along the path facing us.

'What's gone on, exactly,' one of the officers demands as the others head up the garden path towards the front door.

'I used to be married to the man,' I begin, pointing at the house. 'Justin Rose. He was violent and controlling to me. That's his new wife in there. She's laid out on the floor – and so is he – I've no idea what's happened though.'

'And you are?'

'Lynette Rose. I always said it would come to this. I tried to warn you. I don't know how many times I've made reports to you.'

'Where do *you* live?'

'In those flats – number three.'

'And yourself?' He turns to Diane.

'Next door but one. Number nine.' She points in the direction of her house.

'If you could return to your homes while we deal with the situation. We'll be along to get some more details from you shortly.'

He rushes down the path to join his colleagues. An anxious energy hums in the air as the uniform-clad figures gather at the door.

And I'm not going *anywhere.*

40

A POLICE VAN pulls up behind the police cars and spits out a further two officers, each carrying a handle of what looks like a battering ram – the sort of thing I've only ever seen on TV.

'From the presence of this lot, I gather something awful's happened?' I turn to Monica who's the latest neighbour to have appeared.

'You could say that,' I say, my voice bordering on hysteria.

'She might be... gone,' Diane adds. 'And the baby with her.'

'You mean—?'

'I always knew something like this would happen,' another neighbour mutters as she joins us. I recognise her from the opposite side of the square. 'She just kept herself to herself though, didn't she? Instead of reaching out for some help like she should have done.'

I nod. I was the same as Melissa in not asking for support when I was stuck with him. I can empathise with why she stayed. People rarely understand how someone can remain when they're locked in a toxic relationship. Until they're in one for themselves.

The abuse is covert at first. You know it's happened and you're both hurt and bewildered, yet you're led to believe it's somehow your fault too and blame yourself. At the same time, the abuser, seeking forgiveness, reverts to the man he was when you first met him and the cycle begins again. Until the next time.

You're systematically cut off from family and friends until this life becomes your norm and one day, you discover you're on the floor, along with your self-worth and can no longer get back up. I remember the nights of silent tears and the facade of normalcy we put on in public.

Melissa has lived it too.

I'm not the only one who's heard Justin's shouting and Melissa's crying within those four walls since lockdown began. My heart's broken for her, as I've known better than anyone what would probably be taking place behind those constantly-closed curtains.

And now, because no one, including me, has had the guts to do anything dramatic enough to intervene properly, she *really* might be dead in there. If she and the baby die, I don't know how I'll live with myself. I could have done more to protect her, despite my own fear. I *should* have done more.

An ambulance rounds the corner next. As its sirens are silenced, a profound quiet blankets the scene. The officers, masks hiding their expressions, exchange glances, conveying a shared understanding of the gravity at hand as they arrange themselves along the garden path.

I glance from Monica to Diane. We're standing within touching distance of each other – the closest I've been to anyone in weeks. But I'll worry about that later. For now, it feels selfish to worry about catching the virus when Melissa and her baby may well have died in my former home.

'Return to your homes please.' The three of us jump as the voice of one of the officers booms into the street.

But none of us move. Not our little group, or the neighbours who are all creeping forwards from their respective garden gates.

Another officer shouts something but whatever he's saying is diminished by the battering ram as it's hurled repeatedly against the door.

As I wait for it to be forced, I'm inadvertently reminded of when we first moved in here as a family – when Justin carried me across that very threshold – into the house where we were going to have yet *another* fresh start. One where he was going to stop drinking, get some counselling for his anger and hold down his new job.

But within weeks, we'd been back to where we started, only things were even worse than before. One of my greatest regrets is the abuse and violence Cameron was forced to witness over the years. All because I was so ground down that I couldn't say no to giving him another chance. Then another. And another.

I thought I couldn't survive without him when, in all honesty, I couldn't survive *with* him.

I watch as they ram again and again into the door. I feel even more powerless than I've felt all along. This is horrendous.

Each bang against the door strikes at the core of my soul. If she's dead, it's my fault – I didn't act quickly or strongly enough.

Finally, the door crashes open.

The police give way to allow the paramedics in.

A light is flicked on behind the curtains. All we can do is watch what we're unable to actually see.

Each minute stretches out like an eternity. I pace, I perch on the wall, I speak to the other neighbours. The air is thick with shared anxiety. Hands fidget, fists clench, and eyes brim with tears. The consensus is the same. We should have been on the phone to the police morning, noon and night until he was arrested. We should have kept logs of his shouting, all the banging and crashing, Melissa shrieking back at him.

We should have tried harder.

41

SUDDENLY, my attention's drawn to a woman weaving her way through the watching neighbours.

'Melissa. Oh my God. *Melissa*. What's happened?'

'Oh Annie.' Diane steps towards her as though momentarily forgetting herself. She's only stopped as the other woman puts her hands up in an almost defensive gesture.

'Remember where I work,' she warns. 'I don't want to be infecting you.'

'We don't know what's happened yet,' Diane says. 'But they're both unconscious in there.'

'Nooo.' Annie shrieks as she rushes up the path. 'What the hell has he done to her?' Her voice cracks with desperation, echoing our collective fear. She reaches the door only to be swiftly turned back by a couple of the police officers standing guard outside.

'But I'm her friend,' she cries. 'Please tell me what's going on.'

Eventually, after protesting with them for several moments, she returns to us. 'You must know *something*.' She looks from Diane to Monica and then to me.

'She's been really struggling in there,' I begin. 'I've been trying to keep an eye on her from over the way.' I point towards the block of flats. 'But you can only help someone who's willing to let you help them.'

'You must be Simon's new tenant?' She eyes me with an air of suspicion. 'Living in his old flat?'

'That's right.' I take a deep breath. 'And I'm also Justin's ex-wife.'

'You're *Lynette*?' Her voice rises. 'But – but I don't understand. What are *you* doing *here*?'

'The same as everyone else, I guess. Trying to help.'

'Why would you want to live so close to *Justin*? I've heard—'

'I was pretty desperate,' I cut in. 'We were going into lockdown and I had nowhere to stay. And I really mean, *nowhere*.'

The weekend before lockdown was one of the toughest weekends I've ever lived through. I'd only been in my tenancy for three months after a period of sofa-surfing. It wasn't even a proper tenancy.

Because I'd have had no chance of passing a credit check for a letting agent after all the debt Justin had taken out in my name, I'd been forced to contact what turned out to be a very dodgy landlord from a card in the post office window.

But then, just four days before the lockdown announcement, he'd decided to rent the place to someone he knew. Someone willing to pay a lot more than me.

I could have dug my heels in and refused to budge but he made veiled threats of making life very unpleasant for me if I didn't do as he asked. I ended up deciding to cut my losses and just get out. I couldn't live under the rule of a threatening male again – no way.

That Saturday night, I was drowning my sorrows in The Old Crown, deliberating what the hell I was going to do, when Simon offered to let me take his old flat. Yes, it was too close to my old home, but I had no option other than to accept it.

Of course, I could never escape the irony of proximity as my past haunted me from a few doors away. Witnessing the drama over the last few weeks has reopened old wounds, and Annie's presence as Melissa's friend now adds another layer of complexity.

'Melissa never told me you'd moved in.' She frowns as though disbelieving me. 'In fact, she asked if I knew who you were.'

'She never knew about me being Justin's ex.'

'Justin must have told her, surely?'

I shake my head. 'He was hardly going to say, *here Melissa, meet Lynette.* He just wanted me out of there.'

'Simon never said anything to me.'

I shrug. 'I'm sorry if my being here comes as a shock.'

'It's not that – it's just Simon... though to be honest, we've barely had a proper conversation since all this started. I've been too busy working.'

A second ambulance pulls up behind the first and we all look around at each other.

'What's he bloody done to her?' Annie cries. '*What the hell's happened in there?*'

'It's a good sign, surely? A second ambulance, I mean,' says Diane, forever the voice of optimism. 'It must mean they can *both* be saved. They wouldn't be sending two ambulances if there wasn't a chance for them.'

Me and Annie exchange glances. I can tell we're both thinking the same thing without saying a word. *We don't want him to make it. No way.*

'It'll all come out soon enough – whatever's gone on in there,' Monica says. 'Oh my God, *look.*'

I follow her gaze towards the door where Melissa is being carried out on a stretcher, flanked by officers and paramedics who are carrying various machines that are attached to her. An oxygen mask is covering most of her face and she has probes stuck all over her swollen belly.

'Is she going to be alright?' Annie rushes to her side. 'What about the baby?'

'You can telephone the hospital in a couple of hours,' the paramedic replies. 'We're taking her to the Yorkshire Infirmary.'

'I work there,' Annie cries. 'Can't I come with her?'

'I'm sorry. You must know our current protocols. Let us get her stabilised and then—'

'But I'm an intensive care nurse. I—'

'I'm sorry. We need to get her to the hospital and you can call when we get there.'

We watch as she's lifted into the back of the ambulance. Annie sinks to the wall, tears streaming down her face. 'I've been a useless friend,' she sobs. 'I knew what she was going through, yet I've been so wrapped up in work and—'

'Stop it.' Diane sits near her on the wall. I'm surprised one of the officers doesn't tell them to get away from each other but I guess they've got more important things to worry about.

'You've been doing a vital job at that hospital. Melissa told me over the fence, how proud of you she was.'

'Did she?' Annie swipes at her tears.

Diane nods. 'We can't all keep blaming ourselves like this. The bottom line was that she *could* have left him if she'd *really* wanted to.'

'*Something* was keeping her there.' Annie dabs her eyes on her sleeve. 'I could never fathom *what* though.'

'Maybe she saw another side to him,' Monica says as we turn back to the sudden activity at the door. 'Nobody's completely bad, are they? What's that saying, *even a villain loves his mother?*'

They're bringing Justin out. I'm disappointed to see that he's also all wired up and on a stretcher – rather than in a body bag.

He doesn't look to be in great shape though. He's clad in a

vomit-encrusted dressing gown and behind the oxygen mask, his face is grey.

I might have once stood facing the man at the altar and we might have brought a son into the world together, however, I couldn't feel any more disappointed than I do that he's still got a chance of making it.

I really hope he doesn't.

42

<hr/>

It's certainly handy knowing someone who works in intensive care. Without my new allegiance to Annie, I wouldn't be gowned up, masked up and currently making my way to the bedside of my former husband. Not in a million years.

The antiseptic odour assaults my nostrils, mingling with an unsettling scent of fear that hangs in the air. I wonder how many patients on this ward have been admitted with the virus.

Because they've no idea what's caused his toxic reaction, Justin's alone in a side room and as luck would have it, Annie is the nurse on duty and charged with his care today.

As I stand at the door, my eyes meet with my former mother-in-law's over the top of her mask. Annie says Judith has been sitting with him all night. She's asked for me to be allowed in so she can go home for food and a shower.

Taking a deep breath, I walk into the dimly lit room and over to the chair on the opposite side of the bed. As I sit, I can't drag my eyes away from Justin. All I've ever known is a six-foot-two, broad-shouldered and strapping man, but here, he looks almost shrivelled up within that bed. His skin hasn't recovered any of its former colour and Annie tells me that he hasn't regained consciousness since he was brought in over twenty-four hours ago. She has assured me that the outlook doesn't look too promising at the moment.

However, it's difficult not to feel guilty when I look at Judith. Our eyes meet again – mine, dry as a bone – hers, glistening with tears.

'Thanks for coming,' she says, her voice muffled beneath her mask. 'I didn't know who else to ask.'

I want to tell her, *that's because there isn't anyone,* but instead, I say, 'Get yourself out of here and have a break.'

I'd do anything for Judith. She's been good to me and Cameron.

'I feel so guilty,' she says. 'This is the *first* time I've seen him since the two of you split up.'

'You did what you thought was right at the time.' I've often wrestled with the hypothetical scenario of Cameron turning into a violent drunk, wondering if I would respond as Judith did. *Would I turn my back on him?* Cameron's been drinking more and more since starting university, but I can't ever imagine him being aggressive and abusive. Hopefully, my genes have overridden his father's.

My eyes stray back to Justin and all the machines and wires surrounding him.

'What have they said? Is he likely to come through this?' I make a feeble attempt at loading something which sounds like concern into my voice.

'It's still too early to say. It's looking like some kind of toxic poisoning, but they don't know yet what's caused it or how severe it is. They're still doing tests.'

I shiver. It's cool in here after swapping from the heat outside.

'So he couldn't have just done it to himself with excessive alcohol?'

'It's possible. But they just don't know. Not yet.' She follows my gaze to him. 'But no matter what, he's still my boy.' She takes hold of his hand. I don't know whether she's supposed to, what with the virus, but there's no one close by to stop her.

'You do understand that, don't you, Lynette?' She continues. 'No matter how badly he's behaved, he'll always be my son.' She looks at me with watery eyes. 'Sometimes it takes something like this to realise that you *really* do love someone, doesn't it?'

I nod, slowly, and look away. I probably shouldn't be here, yet I couldn't stay away.

'Is there any more news on Melissa?'

'She's still in an induced coma,' I reply. 'While they assess the damage the lack of oxygen might have done.' It's on the tip of my tongue to tell her about the two emptied and discarded inhalers Annie's been told about — one of them was smashed to smithereens after presumably being stamped on.

The police also let on to Annie that if Justin *does* come around from this, they'll be ready and waiting to speak to him. Judith doesn't know about *any* of this yet – *I'm* not even supposed to know. But no doubt she'll find out sooner or later. For now, though, looking at the state of her, she just needs to go home and rest – she looks done in.

'From what that nurse told me before.' I gesture at the door to where Annie's now sitting outside. Her desk's positioned between this room and the next one with a screen at either side of her. I catch her eye through the glass and she offers a faint smile. 'They're going to try and start bringing Melissa around tomorrow.' I hold my hands in the air and cross my fingers.

'That all sounds hopeful.' She turns her attention back to her son as though willing the same sort of promise for him.

'They still don't know whether there could be any brain damage though,' I say. 'No one knows how seriously she was starved of oxygen.' *And it's all because of you,* I say silently in my head as I stare at the rise and fall of Justin's chest.

'It's all in God's hands now.' Judith sniffs and raises her eyes to the ceiling. Then she lowers them back to me and says, 'I'll get going then if that's OK? You'll keep me posted if there's any change with Justin, won't you?'

'Of course I will – I've got my phone.' I tap my gown where it's covering my pocket.

'I do appreciate this, you know. After everything that—'

'It's *you* I'm here for Judith. *Just* you. You've always tried your best with me and Cameron – I know you have.'

A solitary tear escapes her eyes, tracing a silent path down her cheek. 'Thanks love. Look, I know how he was with you, but you will talk to him while I'm gone from here, won't you?'

'Talk to *who*? What do you mean?'

She gestures towards Justin. 'The nurse on duty earlier says he can definitely hear us. I know it all went horribly wrong between you both but you *did* love him once. Surely that must count for something.'

Her voice rises at the end of her sentence as though she's just asked a question as opposed to having made a statement. 'Like I said Judith, I'm here for *you* – *to* give you a break, that's all. I know there isn't anyone else you can ask.'

'I just want him to know he's not on his own, that's all.' Her voice takes on a pleading edge.

'OK, Judith. I'll talk to him.'

'Right, I really *am* going now.' She takes a long look back at Justin as she gets to the door, as though drinking in his every detail. I know what could be going through her mind. *Could this be the final time I see my son alive?*

The door closes silently behind her.

43

I WAIT a few moments for her footsteps to die away along the corridor.

'So, Justin. Apparently, you can hear me.' My voice sounds strange – almost strangled in the beats between the beeping machines.

A surge of bitterness floods my senses, catching me off guard with its intensity.

I glance up to see what Annie's doing – I don't want her to see me *speaking* to him. But she seems engrossed in her phone call. One of her colleagues is sitting at another desk further along the corridor, also in front of two monitors, evidently monitoring her own two patients.

I turn my attention back to Justin – the man who terrorised me for years, now so fragile and vulnerable in his hospital bed. 'You didn't learn after we split up, did you? You didn't learn *anything.*'

The rhythmic symphony of machines echoes through the room, a steady beeping and whirring that punctuates the heavy silence. I wonder what would happen if I were to disable one of them. After all, the very last thing I want is for him to recover. For him to be able to worm around Melissa for another chance if she recovers too.

If they both come through it, Justin will hopefully be convicted, but at the very most, he'd be found guilty of attempted murder, or even just attempted manslaughter, if he has a good solicitor. Even if Melissa dies, life imprisonment doesn't mean life imprisonment any more.

He could be back out of prison in a few years, free to get his hooks into another unsuspecting woman. Free to carry out all the threats he's made to me and Cameron.

'You weren't content,' I continue, 'with how you treated me, were you? After all the busted noses, thick lips and bruises you bestowed, you had to move on and make all your old mistakes over again, didn't you?'

Beneath the lower edge of his mask, his jaw hangs slack. I swear I see him twitch but that's possibly my imagination. He'd be doing more than just twitching if he knew what I'm *really* capable of.

'And with someone pregnant with your child as well.' I lean closer to him. 'I've seen you Justin – I've watched you for weeks. I've seen you pinning her to the ground, sitting astride her, yelling into her face. I've seen you holding her by the throat against a wall. I've heard all your shouting – a sound I thought I'd never have to listen to again. And if that wasn't appalling enough, you thought you could come to *my* door, issuing your nasty threats to me – again.'

I'm on a roll now. 'I *do* hope you can hear me, Justin. I hope my voice is the last thing you ever hear. You're an evil bastard – you don't deserve to have your mother sitting by you, or a son who's still so affected by you. And you certainly don't deserve to play at being a *daddy* again.'

My voice is warm inside my mask as I continue to seethe with my pent-up anger. The last time I was inside a hospital was for stitches several years ago. He'd thrown me out of his way as though discarding a piece of rubbish when I once tried to stop him from going to the pub because it was Cameron's birthday.

I'd landed head-first against the gate post and had been forced to ask Diane to keep an eye on Cameron, who ended up alone on his birthday. At least Justin had been locked up and was safely out of the way.

I was concussed and had to stay at the hospital overnight for observation. I didn't feel strong enough to press charges at the time, even when the police officer who came to see me said that based on witness statements, they could do a victimless prosecution.

However, it all came to nothing, apart from Justin being extra nice to me for a couple of weeks until his build-up-to-explosion cycle started all over again. I've never heard of a man having a monthly cycle but Justin did.

Day one was eruption day when he would engineer a violent row, then he'd spend days two to four in a similar vein, usually away from the house, drinking. Whenever he came home it would be terrifying and these were the times I'd try and get me and Cameron out of the way as much as I could.

Justin would then spend days five to six in a self-pitying state of detoxification, worrying about the damage he might be doing to himself.

This would be followed by several days of him eating well, drinking lots of water, and drinking alcohol more moderately. And I'd hear all his empty promises of how he was planning to change and how everything would be different.

Then his alcohol consumption would increase again, his mood would deteriorate and we'd hurtle towards the day one explosion once more.

'Cameron knows where you are, you know. But he's chosen to keep away from you. How many sons would do that, eh? It just goes to show what an appalling father you've been to him.'

I pause for a moment, my thoughts loud in the silence. I think I'll keep talking so I can drown them out.

'Anyway, you're made of tough stuff, aren't you?' If he *can* hear me, he'll probably like this comment.

'You always boasted that your tolerance to alcohol was like nobody else's.'

I double-check where Annie is before I say what I've got to say next.

44

Annie's still preoccupied out there. Nobody's watching or listening, there's just me and Justin. I can say whatever I want.

'I can't believe how much alcohol you could withstand, to be honest – it should have only taken a day or two to sort you out.'

I swear I see him twitch again. As well he should.

'But we nearly got there in the end, didn't we? And hopefully, we still will. Potent stuff, that methanol.'

I wasn't seeing things when his finger twitched. Something's definitely happening here. One of his legs jerks, then the other. And again. Then his arms. Over and over again. Fear, or maybe, excitement, clutches at my chest. His whole body's convulsing – he's having some kind of seizure.

I watch for a few moments before sweeping my gaze over the displays of the equipment, as if I might have a flicker of a chance of working out what could be going on here.

Eventually, a loud bleeping emits from one of the monitors. I jump out of my seat and rush to the door, if only for the sake of appearances. Annie's still on the phone and the other nurse is nowhere to be seen. I beckon to her. She says something into the phone, places it face down then looks around before rushing towards me.

'Is he having a seizure?' I glance back at him as she passes me in the doorway. *Oh, if you could see yourself now, Justin, thrashing around beneath your sheet.*

'It certainly appears so.' She flicks the switch for the overhead light and dashes to his bed.

'What's happening?'

'It's looking like renal failure,' she says as she hits a button which silences the alarm. 'It's common after a certain degree of toxicity in the system.'

She inspects another machine before darting back to the door and hovering her palm over an alarm button.

But then she pauses and slowly lowers her hand back to her side.

'What are you doing?' I'm as far away from Justin as I can get, with my back against the wall. He's foaming at the mouth and his limbs are jerking in all directions.

'He's seriously ill,' she replies, her tone bearing the slightest trace of panic. 'And likely to die no matter what I do.'

'Likely?'

She nods. 'But if I stall for a moment or two before hitting that button for help, we can swap *likely* to die with *will* die.'

Oh my God. She's on the same page as me. *I knew it.* 'How long will it take?' My voice is almost a whisper.

'I don't know.' Her eyes are wide and terrified above her mask. I wish I'd had a friend like her when I was trapped with him.

I'm torn between my compulsion to leave the room, and wanting to stay and watch the bastard suffer like he's made me and Cameron suffer over the years. The world will be a better place without him, that's for certain, and he'll never be able to abuse another woman.

'Shit, Laura's back at her station. I'll have to do it.' Annie raises her arm, still hesitating, but then, she decisively strikes at the button.

Within seconds, her colleague's running towards the door, followed by a man also wearing scrubs. I get a flash of his badge as he passes me, *Doctor Carl Baines.*

'If you could wait outside please.' He must be talking to me, though he barely looks at me. He's too busy rushing towards Justin as he flails around in his macabre dance, albeit with slightly less vigour than he was a minute or two ago.

'What have we got here?'

I edge from the room, still transfixed on the man who's inflicted so much pain in my life. As the door closes behind me, I can no longer hear what they're all saying, but I can watch them buzzing around Justin like flies, until, as though Doctor Carl Baines senses my morbid curiosity, he strides over and twists the blinds until they shut me out.

I lean against the wall. my mind spinning. I consider heading to the door marked *family room,* even though I'm not exactly *family* any more. Family doesn't do what I've done.

A news article about methanol poisoning planted the seed for my course of action several years ago. But I allowed it to lie dormant. Until I noticed Simon leaving bottles of beer on several of the doorsteps around the square each morning – one of the doorsteps being Justin's. It was then that the seed began to germinate.

After Justin issued his threat to set fire to my flat, the word *methanol* popped back into my head. I got myself online and learned about two of the chemical's most attractive qualities. The first was its ease of availability, the other was the fact that it's indistinguishable from other forms of alcohol. Any methanol in his system would just present like alcohol poisoning, hence foul play would be unlikely to ever be suspected.

I watched for Simon for a couple of days before I made the final decision to execute Justin's exit plan.

Sneaking across the road with my methanol-filled syringe each day, I would additionally leave something like a loaf of bread or a pint of milk so I had a cover story. It would just look as though I was being neighbourly.

My hand would shake as I unscrewed the caps of the bottles to administer my little additive, and I was always poised to run for it if I heard footsteps along the hallway or saw a shape behind the frosted glass.

Throughout my research, I'd learned that just ten to fifteen millilitres of methanol can be more than enough to take out an adult within only a day or two and, as is currently being demonstrated, it isn't exactly a pleasant way to go.

Justin's easily had *triple* that amount over the last two or three days. Simon's been leaving two bottles of beer every morning and I've religiously been over to add five millilitres to each one.

No one knows what I've done, apart from, obviously, Justin himself now. I *wanted* him to know – I promised him when we separated that I'd have the last laugh. He can take this knowledge to wherever it is he ends up.

Any man who threatens to torch my home with me in it, and is capable of emptying the inhalers of his pregnant wife when she needs them, deserves nothing less than what he's got. But it was the threat he made to Cameron about turning up at his university and *forcing* him to listen to what he had to say that got to me the most.

I pace up and down outside the room, eventually sliding myself down the wall to sit on the floor. The stench of antiseptic is turning my stomach. Or is it the stench of death? How long will they work to save him? What will it take for them to decide to give up?

I want to charge in there and say, *just let him die – he deserves to rot in hell.*

45

I DON'T KNOW how much time passes as I sit in a slump. Eventually, the door opens. Disoriented, I stagger back to my feet. It's Annie. I'm relieved she's the person who's come to break whatever the news is.

'What's going on? Is he—?' In this moment I want him to be dead and don't want him to be dead, all at the same time. What I've done is colossal and technically, Justin being dead marks me as a murderer. No matter what he's done in the past, it's a title that will cling to me.

She glances down at the polished white floor before raising her eyes to my face. 'Shall we?' She gestures towards the family room. She's obviously got something to tell me where she feels I need to sit down.

Seated in the sparse room, its clinical aesthetics softened only by a canvas picture of flowers hanging on the wall, Annie and I face each other from the impersonal plastic sofas. She tugs her mask from her face, looking pink-cheeked and sombre behind it.

After an agonising moment, she finally says the words I've been expecting.

'He's dead.' Her voice is flat and matter-of-fact. 'He can't hurt her anymore.'

Or us, I want to add but I stop myself. In the scheme of things, it would make me sound selfish. It might even draw more attention to me in terms of the police investigation. The last thing I want to invite is any unwanted interest. I've used the incognito mode when carrying out my research, but even so, they've probably got ways to get around that and discover *everything* I've looked up. I need to say as little as possible, let them close the case and then I can slip into obscurity and get on with sorting my own life out.

Annie tugs her hat from her head and releases her tight-looking bun so her hair falls around her shoulders. 'My head's killing me,' she says. 'I haven't been getting much sleep.'

I sit back in the chair and let a long breath out. 'Well, I can't say I'm sorry he's gone.' That's the understatement of the century.

'Me neither.' She looks at me with serious eyes. Usually, when she's breaking news of death in this room, I bet it's more challenging than with me. 'About what happened before—'

'We don't have to talk about it.' I look back at her, hoping my eyes portray my sincerity. 'It's between us – you have my word. It'll only ever be between us.'

The air between Annie and me is charged. Sentences hang suspended, filled with unspoken weight. 'He'd likely have died even without me stalling,' she confesses, her words echoing in the room. She closes her eyes. 'After what he did—'

'It's OK – I'm glad you did what you did – you must *never* feel bad about it, do you hear me?'

She scrunches her lips from side to side, conveying an expression which suggests she's going to struggle with what she's done. It's on the tip of my tongue to confess to what put him in here in the first place, if only to alleviate *her* conscience.

But I quickly decide it's a terrible idea.

If I'm to go on with my life, I need to put the Justin chapter well behind me. No one can know – no one can *ever* know. Cameron might proclaim to hate the man, but he's still his father at the end of the day. So no, it's a secret I'll have to carry to my own grave.

An image of Cameron's angry face slides into my mind. He was furious when he found out about their baby on Christmas Eve. If Justin had been a half-decent father to him, it might have been a different story. Instead, he had a childhood of pre-empting his father's mood every time he returned from the pub, as well as suffering his indifference whenever he tried to gain his attention.

Then, as things deteriorated in his teens and he jumped in on more than one occasion to defend me, all hell broke loose. I'll never forget the evening they came to blows and I was forced to call the police. We left soon after that. We should have left much, much sooner, as Cameron often berates me for not doing. But I was as trapped as Melissa seems to have ended up, with my self-esteem on the floor and without the financial means to start again.

Cameron's always been furious that Justin got a second chance at marriage, especially since we heard Melissa seemed not to see his faults or believe anything the neighbours had told her about how he'd treated *us*. Hopefully, she'll get the chance to admit she was mistaken.

'Can I be with you when you break the news to Melissa? I want her to know who I am.'

'You being there might be a bit much for her when she's first told.' Annie's voice softens, as though she's relieved to have moved away from the subject of *what she did*. Or at least, what she thinks she did.

I'd hate for her to be dragging the weight of guilt through the rest of her life. Perhaps, if I can keep an eye on her and we keep talking, I'll be able to convince her that she did the right thing. Or maybe it's better if we never see each other again after I get out of the flat.

'It would really mean a lot to me.' My voice is soft too. In my heart of hearts, I know that seeing Melissa will help me square the circle of what I've done to Justin. It's something that needs to happen as soon as possible – once regret starts to gnaw at me, I'll be done for.

'I'll have to find out if it's what *she* wants. And it will depend on how well she's doing after we've woken her up. It'll take her a day or two to fully come around.'

'We were married to the same monster,' I continue. 'We'll be able to support each other, at least in the beginning.'

'I tell you what.' Annie's expression relaxes. 'I'll keep in touch with you about Melissa's progress, and we'll take it from there. So long as she's OK, I reckon she won't mind seeing you.'

'Fair enough.' I smile at her. There are still hoops to jump through but I feel freer than I have for a long time. 'In the mean-time, I'd better let my son know what's happened to Justin.'

'I'll get in touch with Justin's mum, shall I?' Annie winds her hair back into its band and replaces her hat. Clearly, it's back to business.

'I'll do it.' I close my eyes as I picture the sad face of my former mother-in-law. 'It'll be better coming from me.'

46

I EXCHANGE the cool air of the Yorkshire Infirmary for the heat of the April Day. The sun, casting a warm glow on the hospital grounds, beckons a hope that has eluded me for years. Today, with Justin gone, the possibility of finding pleasure in the simple warmth of sunlight begins to stir within me.

I tug my phone from my pocket and lean beside the wall. I'd like to sit on one of the benches in the sunshine but they're all covered in 'keep off' tape. I can't wait for life to return to normal – these last few weeks have been the longest I've ever known. Especially living in such proximity to Justin and Melissa.

I've got two messages, one from Monica and the other from Cameron. But before I attend to those, I need to call Judith.

She answers on the second ring.

'Oh my God, thank goodness it's only you,' she says. 'For one awful second, I thought it was going to be the hospital.'

I hesitate. I might have hated Justin's guts but I'm still about to tell a mother that her son has died. Her only child. 'They *were* going to call you, but I asked them to let me do it instead. I haven't woken you up, have I?' Like being *woken up* matters in the scheme of things.

'I wasn't sleeping. My brain won't shut off no matter what I do. How's Justin doing?'

The hopeful anticipation in her voice brings tears to my eyes. Yes, I've removed a truly awful individual from this world but I've still robbed a mother of her son.

'Talk to me, Lynette. You're scaring me now.'

'I'm really sorry to have to tell you this, but—'

'*No.*' Her voice cracks. 'Please don't say it. He's going to be alright, I know he is. The nurse this morning said his body just needed to rest and recover.'

Oh, it's going to rest alright.

'I'm so sorry, Judith.'

'No, no, no.' I can imagine her rocking herself backwards and forwards in her lovely bedroom. She has such a beautiful home, one that she's continued to make me welcome at, even since Justin and I separated.

'He died half an hour ago.' I nearly say *passed away* but that sounds too gentle. A vision of him convulsing away in his bed re-enters my mind. I try to blink it away but all that replaces it is a fresh image of him lying on a trolley in the morgue waiting to be sliced and diced. I bet he's been moved there by now. They're so desperate for beds in the intensive care unit that he's unlikely to have been left for long in that single room.

'Half an hour ago,' she echoes.

'The hospital was going to call you straight away but I thought the news would come better from me.'

'Oh my God – Oh my God. My boy – my poor boy.' She's crying now. 'I should never have left him. I knew I was making a mistake the minute I walked away from that room.'

'It wouldn't have made any difference, honestly, it wouldn't.'

'You can't say that. Oh my God.' Her voice is a soft moan. 'I've been such an awful mother to him. I know what he did to you was wrong, but I'm still his *mother*. I should never have cut him off as I did.'

'You did what you thought was right at the time.'

I could spend all day trying to comfort her by saying the right thing but I've got other matters to face. Until the post-mortem has taken place, I won't know whether I can relax or not.

'I don't know what to do,' she cries.

'I'm so sorry, Judith,' I say again. I struggle to find the right words, wishing I could do more to ease the pain I've just unleashed. Did I make the right choice by delivering the news myself? The weight of it presses on my chest.

'I wish you'd stop saying sorry,' she snaps. 'Oh look, now *I'm* sorry. It's just – what's happened is hardly *your* fault.'

I remain silent as she pauses for a moment.

'You did what you could Lynette. You're the *last* person I would have expected to sit at his bedside in his final moments, even if you *were* only there to support me.'

'Is there anyone who can be with you? You shouldn't be on your own at a time like this. I'd offer myself, but I'm going to have to get in touch with Cameron.'

'Of course you are. Let me know how that goes, won't you?' Her voice sounds almost normal again for a moment.

'I will.'

'Tell him I'm here if he needs me for anything. Who knows how the poor lad's going to take the news that his dad's died.'

It might be grief causing Judith's memory lapse but she seems to have forgotten that Justin and Cameron's relationship was hate-filled and non-existent. I hope she's not going to suddenly elevate Justin to some kind of pedestal and try to inflict memories of him onto Cameron whenever they meet in the future.

'You get off the phone and sort Cameron out,' she says. 'I can talk to Millie next door over the fence if I need to. She'll be there for me.'

'Will you be alright?'

'I'll have to be.' She sniffs.

'I'll call you later, Judith. You take care.'

I inhale a jagged breath as I end the call and then tap into my messages.

47

THE FIRST ONE'S from Monica.

> Is there any news? Both me and Diane have tried ringing the hospital but they won't tell us anything.

I deliberate for a moment. Should the news that someone's dead really be broken by text message? Yes, in this case it should. I can't trust my face not to give me away. Not until I've processed and have come to terms with it all.

He died about half an hour ago. I was in the room when it happened.

> Omg – I can't believe he's dead. I know it didn't look good but I thought he'd survive. Are YOU alright?

A bit shaken up by it all but yes, I'm fine.

> The police have been back again, they wanted to know where you were.

Why – did they say?

They asked me a couple more questions about everything so they probably just want to do the same with you.

Have they left a number?

This is a worry. After all, I gave a full statement to them yesterday. What could there be left to ask me about?

I think they posted a card through your door.

Thanks for letting me know. I'll sort it out when I get back.

What's the news on Melissa?

Annie's let me know that she's still in the induced coma but they're going to start waking her up soon.

Well, that's good news. Am I alright to put it into the Facebook group? Everyone's asking after her?

I guess so. It's only the people in the square who'll see it.

How's Cameron?

I'm just about to get in touch with him.

How do you think he'll take it?

Difficult to say. He knew Justin was in intensive care so he's prepared. Anyway – I'll speak to you soon. I need to get on with calling him before he hears the news some other way.

I'm thinking of you. xx

Her last message brings heat to my eyes. If I were to allow myself to cry now though, I'm not sure who or what the tears would be for. Myself probably, and the burden of guilt I've inflicted on myself. I can only pray that it dissipates over time.

The second message is from Cameron.

> I'm in the car park Mum. I'll wait here until you see this message. x

Which car park? Here?

> I couldn't just sit around with all this going on so I decided to drive up. I'm in the multi-storey.

I'll come and find you now.

Breaking into a run, I head towards the multi-storey, all guilt replaced by the thought of seeing Cameron for the first time since Christmas. Part of me was looking forward to a walk back to the square to clear my head, but that's been well and truly replaced by the excitement of seeing my son at last. I don't care if 'the rules' don't permit him to leave his university halls and come back up here. Given what's happened, I'm sure we'd get any fine or whatever other sanction waived by the authorities.

I spot his Fiesta in the corner. He worked every single weekend while he was in sixth form to save for it and get it insured. Though it's slightly battered, it's his pride and joy. I rush over and tug at the passenger door.

'It's so good to see you!' I slide into the seat beside him. 'I want to give you a hug but we'd be breaking the law.'

'Madness, isn't it? Well, you're in this car so we're already breaking the law.'

'Come here you.' I twist in my seat and reach over the gearstick for him. 'I've missed you.'

I don't give a damn about getting the virus at this moment. All I care about is hugging my son.

Cameron's never really been one for hugs and quickly lets me go. 'What's going on in there? I haven't been able to think about anything else.'

I take a deep breath as I look at him. His expression is difficult to read. He never wants to hear it but he's got Justin's dark hair and strong build. His spikey hair grazes against the roof of his car, just like his dad's used to. But he's like me in so many other ways – his eyes, his freckles and thankfully, his temperament – usually.

'OK, I'm just going to come out with it.' I bite at the skin on my lip and close my eyes for a moment.

'What?'

'He died, love.' I glance at the clock on his dashboard. 'Going on for an hour ago.' Like the time of it matters in the scheme of things.

Cameron looks as though he's been winded. 'You're joking, aren't you?' His eyes are wide in his suddenly pale face. 'But he was only in his forties.'

'I know. But the way he was drinking – he was never going to live to a ripe old age, was he?'

Cameron stares at me, shock emanating from his every pore. 'I can't bloody believe it.' He rolls his neck from left to right as if trying to relieve some of his pressure.

'It's OK to be upset, you know.' I reach for his hand but he pulls it away and grabs onto his steering wheel instead. 'Don't worry about what I might think. He was still your dad.'

Seeing his initial reaction makes me even more sure he can *never* find out that I was behind Justin's death. *No one can.*

'It's not that I'm upset as such.' He's gripping the steering wheel so tightly that his knuckles are white. 'It's just – oh, I don't know – I know I should be heartbroken. All my mates at uni would be if it was one of *their* dads. I don't know how I feel.'

'I expect they have mostly *decent* fathers.' My tone is sad, rather than bitter. It's all my fault Cameron had to grow up like he did with a Neanderthal brute he had as his main role model.

It's as though he's read my mind as his grip on the wheel relaxes. 'You did the best you could,' he says.

'I'm so glad you drove up.' I try to smile through tears I didn't even realise I was crying until one plops onto my hand. I'm numb, just so numb, but at some point, I've got to let it all out.

'So am I. The other lads tried to distract me from it all but nothing was ever going to work.'

'I'm not surprised.'

His face brightens which is heartening to see. 'Are you going to show me this flat you're staying in? I'll stay up here for a few days, if that's OK?'

'Of course it is.' Then something occurs to me. 'But it's close to our old house,' I say, pulling a face. 'I mean *really* close. Do you think you can handle that?'

'I've handled much worse, haven't I?' He twists his keys with a sigh and starts the engine. 'Besides, I've nothing to rush back for. That girl I was seeing has buggered off with someone else.'

'I'm sorry to hear that.'

'Yeah, well.' His face darkens and he looks away. It would appear that he doesn't wish to discuss it.

'The police want to talk to me again, so you'll perhaps have to stay out of sight until they leave. I've told them I live alone.'

'I don't give a stuff about the lockdown rules,' he says. 'We've had weeks of being stuck in those halls like prisoners. It's good to be out of there.'

'That's my boy.'

48

CAMERON'S STANDING where I've spent so much of my time in recent weeks – in front of the lounge window – the vantage point I used for keeping an eye on what was happening in our old house. I became adept at being able to pinpoint where Justin and Melissa could be at any given moment, after all, I know that house, probably better than the two of them put together. Having an idea of their routine was particularly useful in the timing of carrying out my beer bottle activities.

'How could you stand living so close to him, Mum?' Cameron twists in the window to face me. Hopefully, he'll stay with me for more than a few days so I can keep a proper eye on him. He changes the subject every time I mention what's happened to Justin and it's difficult to work out what might be swirling around inside him. He's been more preoccupied with drinking beer and constantly messaging on his phone. When I glanced over his shoulder, he seemed to be looking at pictures of some girl on social media – the one he's broken up with, perhaps. I've tried talking to him about her but he swats me away like a fly.

'I *couldn't* stand it if the truth be known.' I lean onto the edge of an unpacked case. There was no point unpacking too much since I don't plan to remain living on the square for longer than I have to. There are too many ghosts here, especially now. 'But you know the predicament I was in – I didn't exactly have much choice.'

'You could have crashed with me. Especially now that Elise has done one.'

'*At your halls of residence?*' I almost laugh at the idea. 'I don't think so.' It's the first time he's mentioned his girlfriend's name though. Maybe he's going to open up to me at last. It might also release the floodgates for him to discuss how he's coping with his father's death.

He looks as though he might retort with something but is stopped as the buzzer echoes through the flat. My breath catches as I stride over to it. It can't be anyone other than the police and I don't know if I'm ready for them yet.

I lift the intercom receiver. 'Yes.'

'Is this Lynette Rose?'

'It is.'

'I'm DC Mark Wilkinson of North Yorkshire Police. Would you be able to come down and speak with us for a few moments please?'

'If this is about Melissa, I gave a statement yesterday.' I need to give off the impression that I've no idea what they could be back here to talk about. I just hope I can keep my shit together. My voice is already wobbling. I glance at Cameron who looks suddenly concerned. He knows me better than I know myself.

'Is it the police?' he mouths.

I nod.

'Yes, it's about the incident yesterday. We've just got a couple more questions to ask you if that's alright?'

'OK – I'll be down in a moment.' I replace the receiver and take a deep breath.

'What do they want?' Cameron asks.

'It's fine – they've got a couple more questions for me, that's all.

But I've got to go down – they're probably not allowed inside anyone's house.' I slide my feet back into my sandals.

'OK.'

'Come away from the window, will you?' I jerk my head towards the sofa, as if to say, *sit there instead, please.*

'Why? I'm only watching what's going on.'

'We're breaking the lockdown rules, aren't we? I don't want you getting sent back.'

'They wouldn't make me, *surely.* Not after what's happened.'

'Most of the neighbours on this square wouldn't have room to talk anyway. I've spent a fair amount of time standing at that window and the amount of rule breakers I've seen...' My voice trails off. Here I am, with the police to face and I'm wittering away about nothing. I'm stalling.

'You'd better get down there, Mum.'

I descend the six blocks of stairs to the entrance door, each step a deliberate move as if trying to postpone my impending encounter with the police.

As I press the button to release the door, I smile at the two officers. Whether or not that's appropriate in the circumstances, I don't know. I don't know how I'm supposed to be behaving or reacting at the moment.

'Thanks for coming to speak to us, Mrs Rose.'

'Call me Lynette,' I say. I don't feel like a *Mrs Rose* any more and don't think it will be long before I revert to my maiden name. The only reason I haven't already is because I wanted to bear the same surname as my son.

'I'm Detective Constable Mark Wilkinson.' The male officer puffs his chest out and then gestures to the woman standing at his side. It's unnerving to note how much he looks like Justin used to when we were younger. From the spiked dark hair to the confident way in which he carries himself.

'And I'm Sergeant Ruth Tomkins.' She nods at me.

She doesn't look old enough to be a sergeant but maybe that's just me getting older.

With nothing better to do at the moment, I bet all the neighbours are curious. I glance around to check. Monica's watching us from her deckchair to the left and the neighbour to my right drops her gaze as soon as I notice her and continues tending to her garden. The officer can hardly send them inside their houses so we can speak privately.

Perhaps they'll want to take me to the police station to question me. Gosh, I hope not – I've come this far and don't want to fall down now. I've never held up well to scrutiny and can't guarantee I won't crumble under the wrong kind of pressure.

'We'll have a wander over to the green, shall we?' DC Wilkinson points in its direction. 'I know it's not very conventional but at least we can speak at a distance from one another.'

'As well as not be overheard,' his colleague says, a little too loudly.

Monica must hear her because she raises an eyebrow as I follow the officers to the gate. I glance up at my window as I close it behind us. Despite me telling him to move away, Cameron's still watching. As I follow the officers, my mind tracks back to how often Melissa and Justin will have glanced up and noticed me standing there – often, over the last few weeks.

We arrive at the edge of the green. Apart from a woman throwing a ball for her dog over at the other side, it's deserted. Without planning to, the three of us arrange ourselves into a triangle. Most people are well-practised in what the prescribed distance apart is now. The situation feels almost surreal and I wonder if I'm the first person they've 'interviewed' in this way.

It's better than being taken to the station, that's for sure. I reflect on the potential dangers, the shortage of face masks, and the confined interview room, heightening the stakes in this unusual encounter.

'What did you want to ask me?' I direct my question at DC Wilkinson since he's done most of the talking so far. Despite the storm of anxiety brewing within me, I manage to keep my voice fairly nonchalant – at least I hope I do.

He clears his throat. 'Just one or two things that weren't addressed in the statement you made to us yesterday.'

I nod as I wait for him to continue.

49

'OK?' *One or two things* doesn't sound *too* bad. However, this will depend on what those *one or two things* are. I see the dog tear after its ball from the corner of my eye. Dogs are one of the beneficiaries of this lockdown. They've got their owners at home all day, they get taken for more walks, they—

DC Wilkinson's voice slices into my thoughts. 'We're aware you've come from the hospital today,' he says.

It's not exactly a question but I nod and wait for him to continue.

'We're sorry to hear the news about your former husband,' Sergeant Tomkins adds.

I'm sure they're both studying me for my reaction. 'Thank you,' I say. *What else can I say?*

'Our first question,' DC Wilkinson begins, 'Mrs Rose, erm Lynette, is to ask why you weren't more specific about the bad blood between yourself and Mr Rose. I'm referring to the statement you initially made to us.'

The handcuffs dangling from his belt glisten in the sun – handcuffs that I pray won't end up being snapped onto me.

'*Bad blood?*'

'We're specifically referring to the allegation of fraud and the court proceedings that have existed between you for many months,' Sergeant Tompkins adds as she brushes a stray blonde hair from her eyes.

That's hardly too sharp a question. I could be alright here. 'I didn't think it was relevant,' I reply. 'Not to what happened yesterday, anyway.' I jerk my head in the direction of my old house.

'The truth is,' he frowns. 'That we still don't know what *did* happen. Not *yet*.' He pauses as though giving me the chance to speak. But I'm saying as little as possible. I'll answer any direct questions and that's it.

'You had quite an acrimonious divorce by all accounts, you and Mr Rose.' DC Wilkinson's tone is almost accusatory and I'm not sure what he's getting at. What I *am* sure of, however, is that I'm going to be the talk of this square for the rest of today. Several of the other neighbours, including Diane, are now watching us from their gardens. So much for me keeping a low profile.

'I guess we did,' I reply. 'Probably worse than most divorcing couples.' Let's see if I can get away with *that* as an explanation. I don't want to get into the specifics of it all unless I have to.

'Given this *bad blood* between the two of you Lynette, why were *you* at his bedside at the time of his passing?' I'm certain that the detective's tone becomes more accusatory, though perhaps I'm being paranoid.

'Justin's still the father of my son, isn't he?' The sun's heat has intensified, and I feel a bead of sweat tracing a path down my forehead, a tangible reminder of the pressure building within. I resist the urge to wipe it away in a futile attempt to maintain composure. 'And I was giving Judith, my former mother-in-law, a break.'

'You must still have a good relationship with her then.' Sergeant Tomkin's face relaxes into a smile which doesn't quite meet her eyes.

'Yes,' I reply. I could go into detail here about how she practically disowned her son and instead supported me, but the less I say, the better. 'She'd been at the hospital all night and needed a break and she didn't want to leave him on his own.'

'So she asked *you*?' Sergeant Tomkins tilts her head to one side as she awaits my reply.

'I don't think there was anyone else she could have asked to be honest. Only close family were allowed in there.'

For a second, I wonder if they'll contradict my reference to me being *close family* since we're divorced. Anyway, that's one question down so far, so if the other is on par with that, I'll be fine.

'The next thing we'd like to ask you about, Lynette...' DC Wilkinson widens his stride as though asserting himself. 'Is regarding some information we've received while taking statements from some of your neighbours.'

I really don't like the sound of this. 'Oh?'

'We've heard this from two different sources – you've been spotted on the porch of the Rose's property on several occasions over the last week. Do you want to tell us about that?'

Bloody hell - I had a nasty feeling on more than one occasion that I was being watched. The square has always been ridiculous for nosying and gossip, but since the lockdown, it seems to be all anyone has left to do.

'Like I already said in my statement, I was looking out for Melissa. Like some of the other neighbours were.'

'*Looking out for her?*' He echoes. 'In what way?'

'Well, we knew things were tough for her in there – with Justin, I mean. I guess with her being pregnant, we felt we should offer support in whatever way we could. So there were two or three of us leaving bits and pieces on her doorstep.'

'Such as?'

'Just things like bread and milk, that sort of thing.'

'If you don't mind me saying...' DC Wilkinson's eyes are marble-hard. 'It seems like a strange thing for an ex-wife to do.'

'I wasn't doing *anything* for Justin – I was only looking out for Melissa.'

'Some might say that's stranger still.' Sergeant Tomkins crosses her arms. 'The ex-wife and the new wife.'

'I don't care what *some might say,*' I reply, hoping the cockiness in my voice doesn't serve to put them against me. 'And I don't see how me trying to help a neighbour and a fellow woman, regardless of who she might be married to, would be relevant to anything.'

'If that's the case, why didn't you tell Melissa who you were? We've heard from other witnesses that she had *no idea* you were Justin's ex-wife.'

Annie must have unwittingly let this slip. I do, of course, have a perfect reason as to why I kept quiet. But if I were to tell them that I've been threatened by Justin over what he might do to me and Cameron if I were to divulge anything, that might cause the police to take an even *closer* look at me when really, I just need them to back off.

'I would have told Melissa *eventually*, of course I would. But there was no way I was going to make things worse by telling her who I was when she was still stuck there, right in the thick of it all.'

'What do you mean?'

'Well I know exactly what Justin's like, don't I? And we'd *all* heard him shouting at her. How many times were *you* called out? I'm sorry to say this but we all failed her really, the police included, by not acting to help her sooner.'

'What's *really* puzzling us though...' DC Wilkinson steps from one foot to the other, seemingly side-stepping what I've just said.

The way he says the word *really* makes me wonder what on earth is coming next. 'Is why the neighbours have told us that you've been spending at least a minute or two on the porch each time you've been there. So why would that be?' He pulls a face as he jerks his thumb in its direction.

'It only takes a moment or two to put a bottle of milk or loaf of bread down on the floor,' Sergeant Tomkins adds. They exchange glances, a silent communication that resonates with an unspoken agenda. They're a real double act, this pair and I don't like them one bit. 'You were said to be bending down in that porch for far longer than just a few seconds. So what were you doing?'

That's easy.

'I was ducking down, like you've alluded to, I'm Justin's ex. I needed to keep myself as far out of sight as possible.'

'But what were you actually *doing*?' His voice is tinged with impatience.

'Listening, that's all.'

'Listening for *what*?' He still looks like he doesn't believe me. So does *she.*

'I was only making sure Melissa was alright.' My face is burning, even though what I've said is partially true.

'You were making sure your *ex-husband's new wife* was alright?' Sergeant Tomkins arches a perfectly plucked eyebrow.

'Not all ex-wives have horns protruding from their heads – and not all ex-wives drip poison every time they speak,' I reply, possibly too glibly. I've done so well up to now and don't want to blot my copybook just as it seems they could be coming to the end of their questions.

After an eternal few seconds, DC Wilkinson steps towards me. 'That'll be all for now then.'

'Really?' My voice is a squeak.

I can hardly believe how painless that was. Thank God for that.

'Clearly, there will be more questions as the investigation proceeds,' he says, his voice stern again. 'We're in the middle of acquiring door-cam footage and local CCTV which might give us more information to piece together Mr Rose's final days and ensure there's nothing we're missing here.'

He doesn't mention anything about a possible post-mortem. But if he's not saying anything, I'm not asking. I expect for the police, deaths are ten-a-penny – especially at the moment. A dead body will be as part of their job as complaining customers are to mine.

'Can I go now?' I shift uncomfortably. The neighbours are all watching from their gardens – they're an audience to a spectacle I never signed up for.

And all I want to do is to hide away until it all blows over.

50

'THANKS FOR SORTING THIS OUT.' I shoot Annie a grateful look. We don't know each other all that well but we've become strangely bonded over the last couple of days with everything that's happened.

Perhaps she's felt *obliged* to pull some strings after what *she* did, in the hope of keeping me on side. She isn't to know that I will *never* divulge a thing. *Never in a million years.* Some secrets can only be buried.

'We can't be too long.' She speaks in a low voice. 'No more than ten minutes. And if anyone asks, you're family.'

'I am – kind of,' I whisper back. 'After all, her baby's going to be my son's brother or sister.'

I follow her through some plastic sheeting and into the High Dependency Unit. It mirrors Intensive Care with its sterile white surroundings, yet the atmosphere is far less deathly and oppressive.

'I'll stay with you, just in case,' Annie says as I follow her under the fluorescent lights and along another corridor.

It's on the tip of my tongue to ask, *in case of what?* But I don't. It's a miracle she's got me in here at all.

'The news has been full of Covid patients abandoned on trollies,' I say. 'At least it's not like that here.'

'You haven't seen it in A and E.' She turns and pulls a face. 'But we're not as bad as other hospitals. Melissa's classed as a vulnerable patient and thankfully, we've managed to get her into her own room.'

'Does she know I'm coming?' We pause outside the room.

'No. I've decided to let you explain who you are if that's OK?' She nods at the nurse at the station, saying, 'We'll just be ten minutes like we agreed.'

She nods back. 'Right you are.'

Annie reaches into a container outside the room and passes me a paper mask. 'Keep this on at all times and make sure there's no physical contact.' She fastens her own to each ear and we head inside.

'I've brought someone to see you.' Annie leads the way across the room and perches on the chair at the side of Melissa. She gestures for me to sit on the other side.

Sunlight bathes the room in a warm glow. But despite the brightness, shadows dance, creating an eerie familiarity, reminiscent of Justin's room just a couple of days ago. For a split second, I see *him*, instead of her, in the bed before me. The realisation of what I've done once again sweeps over me. *I've killed your husband. The father of your unborn baby.* And I realise, to my horror, that I'm shaking.

Melissa looks at me with wide eyes from above her oxygen mask. 'It's *you*.' Her voice is croaky as she points at me.

'Try not to talk too much.' Annie rests a gloved hand on Melissa's arm and in that subtle move, it's obvious how much she cares about her. It's an observation that brings tears to my eyes. Justin cut me off from lots of my friends when we were still together and I've never recovered from it. 'Let Lynette do the talking.'

'*Lynette?*' Melissa tries to sit up.

'I'm here to explain myself.' I speak quickly, in case she's having any thoughts of preferring me to leave. 'Justin was just as awful to me as he's been to you.'

'I know.'

As I sit before Melissa, the air crackles with unspoken words. Our gazes lock – a silent acknowledgement of shared wounds. In this fragile moment, we are allies, bound by the legacy of a man who revelled in trying to tear our lives apart.

'Melissa's had the news of his death,' Annie says.

Tears fill her eyes. 'I feel so guilty.'

'What on earth for?' Annie's voice lifts as she squeezes Melissa's arm. 'He was the guilty party – not you.'

I swallow, knowing full well Justin would still be alive and kicking if it wasn't for *me*.

'Are you *really* her?' Melissa's red-rimmed eyes survey me. '*Justin's ex, Lynette?*' My eyes fall on the bruising up her skinny arms. *My* arms used to look like hers. He was an absolute *brute*.

'Yes. And I'm sorry you've only just found out.'

'But, why did—'

Her voice trails off as Annie nudges her. 'You need to rest,' she says. 'Just listen and try not to talk.'

'You're probably wondering what I was doing, living in that flat so close to you both?'

She nods, so I continue.

'I had nowhere else to go,' I say. 'Obviously, it was far from ideal, but I was desperate. We were about to lock down and I'm in a pretty precarious financial situation, thanks to...' It's my turn for my voice to trail off. I can't even bear to say the man's name anymore. 'Do you know about the debt he put me in?'

'I do now.'

'Within hours of getting my stuff in there,' I continue. 'I realised from what I was seeing and hearing that *he* hadn't changed one bit. He was back to his old tricks, but with *you* this time.'

My eyes fall on the shape of her belly, swollen beneath the sheet and I'm hit with a fresh wave of resolve. Perhaps without doing what I did, that baby wouldn't have had a chance in life. At least I've given the kid the opportunity to grow up in a peaceful home, surrounded by love instead of toxicity.

'I knew from Cameron that you were expecting,' I go on. 'But even without knowing that, I'd have worried about you being trapped in the house like you were. The man's a total animal.'

'*Was* a total animal.' Annie stares down at the floor. It's clear she's blaming herself for his death. I'd love to put her out of her misery and tell her of my involvement but I just can't risk it.

'Is that why you were watching me?' Melissa's voice sounds raspy and pained. 'Because you were worried?'

I nod. 'I can't tell you how powerless I felt. A few of us wanted to help – some of us tried. But what with the virus and then with him being so—' I stop myself from carrying on. I *can't* head down this line of explanation. Like when I spoke to the police, I need to keep quiet about the threats he made. There's been enough neighbour and police attention on me as it is, without inviting more.

At least no one seems to have told the police *anything* about him shouting and carrying on in my garden the night before he died. It still feels miraculous, but *maybe* only Melissa heard and saw anything that night. I feel certain our nosy neighbours would have imparted their observations straight away if he'd woken them.

'Have *you* said anything to the police? About him being in my garden that night, I mean.'

'Why would I? I thought you were having an affair with him.' Melissa's voice is barely audible.

Annie frowns at her as if to say, *stop speaking and rest.*

'No chance.' I could almost laugh at this. 'He was trying to warn me off.' I need to play this down. 'He was furious that I'd moved in across the way and that he was right under my nose. You know how controlling he was. I'd have been the *last* person he'd want getting anywhere near you with the truth.'

'Melissa *had* already seen the light.' Annie crosses one leg over the other. 'She *was* planning to leave him but then lockdown happened.'

'Really?'

She nods.

'From what I can gather,' Annie continues. 'You did as much as you could. You even put *yourself* at risk, trying to help Melissa.'

'Ah, but I was used to him, wasn't I?' Restlessness courses through me, and I shift in my seat. The creak of the chair echoes in the otherwise quiet room. 'He couldn't threaten me with anything I hadn't heard before. Plus I was at more of a safe distance and usually behind a locked door.'

'Five minutes please.' The nurse from the station outside pokes her masked face inside the door.

'OK,' Annie nods, looking at Melissa. 'She's getting tired anyway.'

'Look, Melissa.' I need to say this before I get kicked out. 'I came here today to say how sorry I am. I *didn't* do enough to help you – things should never have gone as far as they did. I'm just so relieved you and the baby are going to be alright.'

'Touch wood.' Melissa reaches for her head and her eyes crinkle up at the corners. Behind her mask, I'm certain she's smiling.

Annie looks pensive. 'Me and Simon should have just dragged you out of there – virus or no virus.'

'I've been lucky,' she whispers. 'But I don't know what I'm going to do after here.'

'I've some idea what you're going through,' I say. 'And I want to help if you'll let me. We can get each other through this.'

She seems exhausted as she looks from me to Annie. 'I *am* really tired,' she says. 'But I appreciate you coming to see me.'

'Thanks for letting me in. I'm sure you'll have heard a ton of nasty stuff about me – I wouldn't have blamed you if you'd told me to take a running jump.' I laugh but it sounds hollow as it reverberates around the walls.

Melissa shakes her head as she closes her eyes.

We're nearly at the door when she suddenly raises her head from the pillow. 'Hang on Lynette?'

We both turn back. 'What?'

'I'll never forget what you did. And don't worry, I'll never say a word to the police.'

Something inside me runs cold as her cryptic assurance hangs in the air. I can't even reply to her.

She closes her eyes again and leans back against the pillow.

'What did she mean?' Annie says as we find ourselves back in the corridor.

I shrug. 'I've got absolutely no idea.'

If Melissa *does* know what I was doing to Justin's beer, she'd be complicit in his death for not speaking up to prevent me. Therefore my secret *should* be safe.

'She's probably confused,' Annie says as she leads me towards the main exit. 'She's been through a significant trauma – not to mention the drugs she's on to help her recover.'

So it seems there are *three* of us with Justin's blood on our hands.

Which only goes to show what an abominable human being he was.

MELISSA

EPILOGUE

> How's my favourite friend? xx

> We're all good thanks. Hope you're having a more peaceful morning than we are!! xx

> I love you all loads. Give those kids a big squeeze from me! xx

I PLACE my phone on the coffee table and smile. Annie religiously texts me every morning now – whether she's on shift or not. Despite me repeatedly trying to reassure her, she's never quite forgiven herself for not keeping more of an eye on me when we went into lockdown.

I've never quite forgiven myself for burying what I know about *her* husband, but I've decided it's for the best if I do. I have, however, taken the liberty of cornering Simon with a little ultimatum of my own – that if he *ever* betrays my best friend again, I'll tell her *everything*. That's *after* I've chopped his balls off, of course.

Aisla storms in, her fiery red hair a vivid declaration of her anger. 'Mum, Ewan's being mean to me,' she huffs, eyes ablaze.

Ewan scoots in, ready to defend himself. 'She's lying. I only said—'

'Honestly, you two.' I smile at them. I don't think I've told them off *once* since I got them back from Rick and Cara, and I don't intend to start now. 'You just need to get logged in and ready for your teachers. If you do as you're told, we'll do some baking later.'

'Yesss.' And off they go again.

I reach into the carrycot for Layla, smiling as she curls her fist around my little finger. I was worried she might look like Justin but thankfully, I've only ever been able to see her big sister in her.

I pick her up and lay her against my shoulder. 'You're mummy's little star, aren't you?' I whisper. Layla's entrance into the world, five weeks early, felt like a whirlwind – a mix of fear, hope, and the undeniable strength of my tiny miracle.

Our terraced house, nestled on this quiet street, emanates all the charm of a new beginning. The cosy living room, filled with everything I've missed over the last few months, has granted us a fresh start.

If things had been different and we'd got ourselves in here on that first day of lockdown, would Justin still be alive now? Probably. But would he be leaving me alone and allowing me to get on with bringing up my kids in peace? Probably not.

Layla nuzzles into me and I say a silent prayer that we've come through relatively unscathed. Rick and Cara offered to keep the children a while longer so I could get settled in here but I said no and took them back the moment I could.

Aisla and Ewan loved helping to get the new house ready, though I thought I'd have longer to spend with them on their own, making up for nearly three months without them. However, Layla had other ideas when she decided to make an early appearance.

The schools are gearing up for phased returns this month, promising a semblance of normality. But normality, like everything else, comes tinged with echoes of the past. My days will be filled with keeping them organised, taking care of Layla, visiting Mum and continuing to get myself back together. My counsellor's reduced our online sessions to weekly ones so at least I'm heading in the right direction.

As the children settle to their work, one in the lounge and the other in the kitchen, the postbox rattles. Every noise it makes sends shivers down my spine, but I've learned to breathe through it. No longer a reminder of Justin's rage, it's just a letterbox now.

The envelope, bearing news of our old house being listed for sale, feels like a bittersweet echo. I flip through the attached photographs, each one a haunting reminder of a life I've left behind. On the surface, the house appears to be a perfect family home, ready and waiting for love and laughter to infiltrate its walls. When we move into a house, that's all we can ever hope for.

I hoped for that, and before me, so did Lynette. But as we've both found, the choice of life partner makes or breaks what sort of a home you have. Justin came close to breaking us – both of us.

The equity of the house will cover the debts he ran up and if there's anything left, me and Lynette are going to split it between us.

She endured a nightmare after Justin died as the police prodded and poked around, rather than accepting the cause of death as given on Justin's death certificate – *death from disease related to chronic alcohol use.*

The fact that it took over a month before he could be cremated was also hard to bear. The two of us needed closure so badly that when it finally came, it was like the final chapter of a dark novel, and felt like a rock had finally been rolled back from where it had been squashing us into the ground.

There were only four attendees at his funeral, the celebrant, Judith, Lynette and Cameron who, according to Lynette, turned up drunk. I couldn't have gone anywhere near it but Lynette said her reason for attending was to make sure he had *definitely gone*. She was surprised at Cameron's wish to be there and has been worried about what might be going on in his head since he lost his father and split up with his girlfriend. She says he clams up whenever she tries to talk to him about any of it.

Judith had wept for her only child, not only because that's what a mother does, but somewhere within her, she'll probably still feel responsibility for having exposed Justin to his violent father. She'll know in her heart of hearts that it went on for longer than it should have. I can hardly judge her for this – I exposed my children to Justin's behaviour as well and even a few months of it was a few months too many.

Lynette was an unexpected ally in my darkest hours. I can barely believe the thought of Justin having *an affair* with her even crossed my mind that night. Our friendship has certainly raised a few eyebrows amongst those who discover our history. Cameron also thinks it's a bit weird and has been having trouble warming to me and my kids, especially Layla. Despite what anyone thinks, mine and Lynette's friendship is one I can imagine becoming long-term. She looked out for me at a time when I needed somebody and I'll never forget that.

Perhaps one day I'll be able to tell her exactly what help I witnessed her giving me on the final day of Justin's life – what I saw her doing via the spy hole in my front door.

Though perhaps now, for all our sakes, it's best to say nothing at all and just get on with the rest of our lives.

As I place the photos from the estate agent in the drawer of the sideboard, my phone beeps with a number I don't recognise.

> My father was right. You women are all the same.
> You should have died, not him.

I glance at Ewan, immersed in his Maths, hoping and praying that I got him away from Justin before his rot had *any* chance to worm into him. Unlike it has with Cameron.

The apple, it seems, hasn't fallen very far from the tree.

Before you go...

Thanks for reading Lockdown - I really hope you enjoyed it!

If you want more, visit Amazon to find out more about Frenemy where you'll meet Dastardly Donna - I can't wait to find out what you think of her!

And for a FREE novella, please Join my 'keep in touch' list where I can also keep you posted of special offers and new releases.

BOOK CLUB DISCUSSION QUESTIONS

1. Cases of domestic abuse surged during lockdown. What do you think were the biggest reasons for this?

2. Though Melissa feared Justin, she feared the virus more. Explore what her state of mind must have been like in coming to this conclusion.

3. Was the children's father Rick justified in how he dealt with the situation? How could he have handled it better?

4. How did Melissa's character evolve throughout the story? What strengths or weaknesses did you observe in her?

5. In what ways did the lockdown intensify the challenges Melissa faced in her abusive marriage?

6. How was the backdrop of a national lockdown used to heighten the tension in the story? In what ways did the external pandemic mirror or contrast with Melissa's internal struggles?

7. Discuss the theme of coercive control and manipulation in Melissa's relationship with Justin. How did the lockdown exacerbate these dynamics, and were there moments when you felt Melissa could break free?

8. Explore the role of Melissa's neighbours and friends in the story. How did their attempts to reach out impact the narrative?

9. How did Melissa's fight for freedom reflect the depths of human resilience? Were there moments that particularly stood out to you in showcasing her determination to survive?

10. How did the book make you feel? Were there scenes that particularly resonated with you?

11. Discuss your thoughts on the resolution of the story. Were you satisfied with how the book concluded, and did it leave you with lingering questions?

FRENEMY - PROLOGUE

I step back from the door, peering up at the house. The upstairs is in darkness, but the flickering TV is visible between the cracks of the blind. Is she *hiding* in there? Ignoring the door? She wouldn't have known I'd be calling tonight, so it can't be that.

I lift the flap of the letterbox and peer inside. Nothing. I check up and down the street. Deserted. I brush beads of sweat from my brow before creeping around the side of the house, picking my way through the bins and stepping over plant pots. The gate creaks as I push it open.

Curtains curl out of the open patio doors. As I start in that direction, my attention is diverted to a dark shape at the side of the shed.

It's... She's...

I drop into a crouch beside her. I reach for her hand. As my fingers search her wrist, I see a halo of darkness surrounding her head. Blood. Her hair flutters in the breeze. Her eyes stare back. Dead.

Find out more on Amazon

INTERVIEW WITH THE AUTHOR

Q: Where do your ideas come from?

A: I'm no stranger to turbulent times, and these provide lots of raw material. People, places, situations, experiences – they're all great novel fodder!

Q: Why do you write domestic thrillers?

A: I'm intrigued why people can be most at risk from someone who should love them. Novels are a safe place to explore the worst of toxic relationships.

Q: Does that mean you're a dark person?

A: We thriller writers pour our darkness into stories, so we're the nicest people you could meet – it's those romance writers you should watch...

Q: What do readers say?

A: That I write gripping stories with unexpected twists, about people you could know and situations that could happen to anyone. So beware...

Q: What's the best thing about being a writer?

A: You lovely readers. I read all my reviews, and answer all emails and social media comments. Hearing from readers absolutely makes my day, whether it's via email or through social media.

Q: Who are you and where are you from?

A: A born 'n' bred Yorkshire lass, with two grown up sons and a Sproodle called Molly. (Springer/Poodle!) The last decade has been the best ever: I've done an MA in Creative Writing, made writing my full time job, and found the happy-ever-after that doesn't exist in my writing - after marrying for the second time just before the pandemic.

Q: Do you have a newsletter I could join?

A: I certainly do. Go to https:www.mariafrankland.co.uk or <u>click here through your eBook</u> to join my awesome community of readers. I'll send you a free novella – 'The Brother in Law.'

ACKNOWLEDGMENTS

Thank you, as always, to my amazing husband, Michael. He's my first reader, and is vital with my editing process for each of my novels. His belief in me means more than I can say.

A special acknowledgement goes to my wonderful advance reader team, who took the time and trouble to read an advance copy of Lockdown and offer feedback. They are a vital part of my author business and I don't know what I would do without them.

I will always be grateful to Leeds Trinity University and my MA in Creative Writing Tutors there, Amina, Martyn and Oz. My Masters degree in 2015 was the springboard into being able to write as a profession.

And thanks especially, to you, the reader. Thank you for taking the time to read this story. I really hope you enjoyed it.